PRAISE FOR ZARA ALTAIR

A cracking yarn that wears its deep research lightly...
— CLARISSA PALMER

Leaves you wanting more!
— DAVID AMERLAND, AUTHOR

This series would make an excellent show!
—JOE MCGAHA, WRITER/PRODUCER

THE VELLUM SCRIBE

An Argolicus Mystery

ZARA ALTAIR

ISBN: 978-1-7327225-0-7

❀ Created with Vellum

INTRODUCTION

Thank you for reading *The Vellum Scribe*.

Join the Fans of Argolicus. Get a free guide to some great historical novels. And, I'll send you personal updates about the Argolicus Mysteries

Discover more at the end of the book. Ostrogoth is a term created by historians centuries after the reign of Theodoric. They referred to themselves as The People. Their language was Our Language. Their church, Arian in nature and established before the Council of Nicea, was Our Church.

At the time of the story, monks both Arian and Trinitarian either lived alone or in loose communities based on the tradition of the Desert Fathers like Anthony. At this time, Benedict lived alone in a cave following that tradition. He had yet to form his monastery or create his Rules. Of course, his connection with Lucas comes from my imagination.

Modern readers should understand that religion and politics were intertwined. Feelings ran high about the nature of Christ and colored daily activities and interactions in a way it's difficult to comprehend today.

The Henotikon was a document issued by the Emperor Zeno in 491 C.E. in an attempt to unify the various sects (heresies) of the Christian church. It caused a schism between East and West and was not settled until 519 C.E. seven years after the time of this story.

To the Trinitarian Church in Constantinople, Argolicus and his uncle, Wiliarit, were heretics.

ENTER THE WORLD OF ARGOLICUS

With few exceptions, the western world was at peace in the year 512 after Christ's birth. Warlords were plotting in the Balkans either for the East or the West, but mainly for their own power. Rumblings in Persian borderlands perhaps threatened the Roman Empire as seated in Constantinople. The most recent disturbances—betrayals, if you will—of the Frankish kingdoms had been settled some five years. Bishops and clergy squabbled over textual interpretations of the Gospel, patristic writings, or Patriarchal proclamations, as usual, some in a huff, others with conciliatory leanings. Vandals had controlled northern Africa for almost 100 years. The Visigoths ruled Spain and traded with avarice. In Italy, affairs of concern were mainly internal—the parallel Roman law and Ostrogoth legal systems ran under the regal Edicts guided by a sense of civility, providing structure for dispute resolution.

CHAPTER 1
ARRIVAL

T he patrician, Argolicus, dropped his practice sword when he heard his mother cry out. He ran from the courtyard to the front of the villa followed by his sparring partner and tutor slave, Nikolaos.

A cart stood in front of the villa at the end of the road that came up from the town of Squillace. The Ionian sea shone blue in the early morning March sun. The carter unloaded several wooden boxes, carefully placing each one on the ground. Argolicus heard his mother laugh and saw her long blond braid covered by thick arms. A large man in a plain brown robe held her close in a tremendous hug and then pushed her away.

"Uncle," Argolicus cried in Their Language. His face broke out in a spontaneous smile.

The big man turned. "Argolicus. The Father and the Son together!"

"Worship and glorify," Argolicus responded. "Uncle Wiliarit, where have you been this time?" He embraced his uncle who reciprocated in a hearty hug, squeezing him into the large chest.

Wiliarit continued in the language of The People, "I've been in Constantinople working on a commission. But now I'm here to finish and I'm hoping Nikolaos will help."

Nikolaos heard his name and came closer, still clutching his practice sword. Besides keeping Argolicus in practice with arms, he was an excellent grammarian and had taught Argolicus Greek since childhood. But, his language skills stopped at the tongue of King Theodoric and his people.

"Nikolaos?" Argolicus replied. "Yes, it's a medical reference book. He knows much about plants and herbs. I'm hoping he can point out some live specimens for illustrations. What I have now as a source are drawings in another manuscript. I want this one to be as excellent as possible. It is quite a large commission."

୬ℛୄ

Argolicus put down his pen and knife and looked up from his calligraphy of The People's language when he heard Nikolaos calling his name from outside the villa. Wiliarit, his uncle, had chastised his nephew for not practicing writing and had set him to calligraphy with the language of The People—the king's People, Wiliarit's People, his mother's People, his People. He glanced down at his work and frowned at his lack of skill. Wiliarit was right. Neglect was obvious.

But now, Nikolaos was closer and his calls were urgent. "Master! Master!" He arrived panting in the study.

"What is it? I thought you were looking for flowers." Argolicus said, standing up from his table.

"We are. We were. But down in the Angel's Meadow there's a body. Come." Now, his tutor was out of breath.

"A body? Do you mean someone is dead? A dead body?" Argolicus shook his head.

"Yes, yes, a very dead body. His face is blue. The skin..." His face distorted as he searched for words and then gave up. "You must come and see."

Argolicus nodded, reached for his cloak on a chair, shouldered it against the cool late March air, and followed Nikolaos along a maze of animal trails over a hill to a verdant meadow. Here and there wildflower colors - yellow, purple, blue, red - protruded among the green of early grasses.

Wiliarit stood in his dark brown robe in the middle of the meadow, ignoring his unopened box of paints and vellum sheets beside him. His head was bowed and his arms uplifted in prayer. They waited for him to finish. When he concluded, Wiliarit lowered his arms, raised his head, and turned toward Argolicus.

"Alone...without a burial." Wiliarit shook his head. "And his head—who would do such a thing?"

Argolicus walked toward the body. Dark hair covered his head but the skin was dark blue. Mottled arms of orange and red skin tones poked out from an old linen tunic. A wool cloak lay crumpled under the body. The odor of rotting flesh permeated the cold air. Argolicus noticed the concave wound on the skull and knew the cause of death.

"Days," he said. "He's been here many days. A week? Maybe." Sunlight glistened off a ring submerged in a bloated finger—a circlet of gold with one dark ruby. "I know that ring." He turned to Wiliarit. "Do you remember Lucas?"

Wiliarit nodded. "Yes, so sad. That was a hard lesson for you."

"Lucas? The son of Bartholomaeus?" Nikolaos asked. "That Lucas?" He moved closer to Argolicus and the body and peered down.

"It wasn't his fault our friendship ended," Argolicus said. "It was his father. His father didn't want him near a heretic like Wiliarit. Remember all the antagonism toward Our Church and the threat Wiliarit posed to his son's true faith? Father was a Roman. With Father, a Roman, gone, Wiliarit's influence was anathema. The Nature of Christ is always a contentious point, especially here in the South. Lucas came one last time to say goodbye even though his father forbade his seeing me."

"He was a better swordsman than you," Nikolaos said. "But what is he doing here? Why doesn't his family miss him?

I've heard nothing about his being missing among the slave gossip."

Argolicus stood. "We must tell the family. Nikolaos, go back and tell Lucius or whoever is in the stables to get horses ready."

"I'll stay here by the body and paint," Wiliarit said. "As I remember, I would open old wounds. That would just add to the old man's sorrow."

"Closed minds seem to stay closed." Argolicus said. He sighed. "We wouldn't want to open those old wounds now." He turned toward the disappearing Nikolaos and shouted, "Two horses. Just two."

Wiliarit looked at his nephew. "I know you are a grown man now, but do you think it is wise to see that family?"

"They have to know about Lucas. Being direct is always the best action in the long run. I'll deliver the news and leave."

Wiliarit nodded. "Go in peace. I'll just sketch that little red flower. I've forgotten what Nikolaos said it was, but he can tell me later."

"What do you mean Lucas?" Bartholomaeus asked. A man in his late fifties, his voice filled the room as he glowered at Argolicus. His face was long, accented by a prominent hooked nose. "In Angel's Meadow? He's in Rome, or, he was leaving Rome to visit a monk in the mountains. Someone named Benedictus. You must be mistaken."

Argolicus stood in the atrium of the large villa of Vibius Horatius Bartholomaeus, whose money supported the local church. The midday sun shone through the opening above onto the rich mosaics on the floor and highlighted the man's silk robes. His biblically named sons, Matthaeus and Marcus, stood next to him cast from the same mold—dark hair, sturdy medium build, and a permanent frown. The surrounding walls were painted in bright colors and frescoes of saints, richly adorned, but saints. Argolicus knew even though he was equal in standing, religious affiliation to the Trinitarian doctrine held more power here than it did in Rome. Not all Christians were equal here, no matter how much King Theodoric had proclaimed tolerance and cooperation in his rule of *civilitas*. This family held the local power because of their support of the Church. But, whatever the staunch religious antagonist had to say, Argolicus knew Lucas was the dead man in the meadow.

"I recognized his ring. And even in death, I recognized my friend," he said, keeping the topic focused on the dead body and not religious debates.

"Stop. Stop right there. He is... was... not your friend. Get out of my house with your barbarian tricks." Bartholomaeus put up his hands as if to ward off Argolicus. His gesture denoted abhorrence rather than an order to leave.

"I will leave here to notify the bishop, so the man will have a burial. He was bludgeoned with a club or large branch. He deserves Christian care."

Bartholomaeus scowled. "Father, Argolicus is right," Marcus, the younger son. said, "Our first concern is to care for Lucas." He turned to his sister, Maria, dark-eyed and lithe. "Get people ready to receive his body. We will prepare him here."

Maria looked at Marcus, then her father, and gave a tearful, beseeching look to Argolicus before she turned to find the servants. Her soft leather shoes padded across the marble mosaics as she headed toward a hallway.

"Our bishop, Braga, will serve all of our funeral needs," Matthaeus said, his frown an echo of his father's dark glower.

"Now, you can leave." His silks whispered as his arm swept the air in a dismissive gesture toward the entry.

"Matthaeus, wait," Marcus said, stopping his brother. "I will go with Argolicus to bring back Lucas." He turned to Argolicus. "I'll meet you in front. I'll bring slaves and a cart."

Argolicus took in the three men and nodded at Marcus. "Your Sublimity," he said to Bartholomaeus. He turned toward the entryway and strode across the grand room to the vestibule. Nikolaos trailed behind.

In the vestibule before the large entry doors, Maria emerged from a small room. Once again, her brown eyes beseeched. "Wait," she said. "I want to talk to you. They are lying." She pressed a small folded piece of vellum in his hand and scurried away.

When Marcus arrived outside, he rode alongside Argolicus as Nikolaos and a cart with six slaves to load the body trailed behind. His bearing was not as aggressive now that they were away from the villa.

"You have to understand that my father's faith keeps him from seeing the big picture."

"My friendship with Lucas is part of that big picture he missed," Argolicus said. "I know now that people come and go in life, but Lucas was a friend, a part of my youth."

"Your friendship started my father's disapproval of Lucas. My brother was always a bit of a rebel and Father wanted to quell his differences."

"His differences? When we were together, he was a normal boy—running, climbing trees, shooting arrows. What is different about those things? You are supporting your father's ideas without looking at what was happening. We never once talked about religion. We were boys exploring the world." Argolicus felt his anger grow as he tightened his grip on the reins. Marcus was an adult. Why didn't he form his own opinions?

Marcus shifted in the saddle. Nikolaos behind them and the slaves on the creaking cart all were silent in the way that collected gossip and then sent it everywhere.

"It was your uncle. After your father died," Marcus paused to cross himself, "Your uncle came to stay. Father was horrified at the prospect of a monk of your faith, influencing Lucas. Lucas was heartsick when Father cut your connection. It was as though his youth stopped then. He became withdrawn. He didn't share much of what he was doing. His presence was like a black cloud. None of us were sorry to see him go when he left for Rome."

Argolicus felt sorrow grip his heart. He had lost a playmate and friend. At the time, his family and his friend, Cassiodorus, Senator, had filled his life. Lucas had found no people to fill his life. Instead, he had drawn away. They rode in silence toward the meadow.

CHAPTER 2
THE BODY AND THE SOUL

he wagon creaked to a halt in the meadow as Wiliarit turned with a somber face and began putting his brushes and paint pots into his box. The midday sun had warmed the air and though more wildflowers had opened sprinkling colors throughout the emerging green grass the odor of the decaying corpse filled the meadow.

Marcus dismounted and inched up to his brother's body. He looked, bolted back, and then turned, vomiting over the fresh flowers in the grass. A slave ran up to offer him a cloth. He wiped his mouth, took a deep breath, and turned back toward what remained of Lucas' body. He stared open-mouthed gasping for air. He crossed himself three times and then raised his hands, palms up, and began to pray. "Blessed is our Lord God, always; both now and ever, and to the ages of ages."

The slaves around the cart raised their hands and stood mute as they listened to his prayer until the end when they joined in to recite, "Lord, have mercy," twelve times. Marcus put down his hands and looked at Lucas' body.

"His face. His face," Marcus said. "It's dark as a devil. Is this what happens when the soul departs?"

Wiliarit opened his mouth, but Argolicus frowned, waving his hand to stop him. He walked up to Marcus. "Being outside exposed to the sun has hastened the dissolution of his body."

"He was beautiful," Marcus said. "Now everything about him is disgusting. My baby brother has turned into a monster.

I will never get rid of this sight in my head. Never." He turned away to vomit again. When he recovered, he pointed to the bloody depression in Lucas' head. "Who would do this?"

Argolicus remembered Maria's warning. He wondered what she had meant about lying. And who were they? Did she mean the father and the brothers? If so, Marcus might be feigning. The decomposing body was repulsive. Even if Marcus had killed his brother, the sight of the body days later was enough to disturb anyone. And, if Marcus were the killer, then the decomposition could prompt not just revulsion but guilt.

"We could speculate, but that is all it would be," Argolicus said. "Now is the time to take care of Lucas. Get him home or to the clerics to prepare his body for burial."

Marcus nodded and made the sign of the cross three times. "You are right. The sooner he is in the ground, the sooner this ghastly vision will be gone."

Argolicus probed. "Can you think of who would want to do this?"

"My brother," Marcus said. "Father is angry at him, as you saw, but he...he wouldn't do that to anyone. He is strict and blunt but not vengeful. In his own way, he cared about Lucas. Lucas was going off with no prospects. He wanted to support joined in to recite, "Lord, have mercy," twelve times. Marcus put down his hands and looked at Lucas' body.

"His face. His face," Marcus said. "It's dark as a devil. Is this what happens when the soul departs?"

Wiliarit opened his mouth, but Argolicus frowned, waving his hand to stop him. He walked up to Marcus. "Being outside exposed to the sun has hastened the dissolution of his body."

"He was beautiful," Marcus said. "Now everything about him is disgusting. My baby brother has turned into a monster.

I will never get rid of this sight in my head. Never." He turned away to vomit again. When he recovered, he pointed to the bloody depression in Lucas' head. "Who would do this?"

Argolicus remembered Maria's warning. He wondered what she had meant about lying. And who were they? Did she mean the father and the brothers? If so, Marcus might be feigning. The decomposing body was repulsive. Even if Marcus had killed his brother, the sight of the body days later was enough to disturb anyone. And, if Marcus were the killer, then the decomposition could prompt not just revulsion but guilt.

"We could speculate, but that is all it would be," Argolicus said. "Now is the time to take care of Lucas. Get him home or to the clerics to prepare his body for burial."

Marcus nodded and made the sign of the cross three times. "You are right. The sooner he is in the ground, the sooner this ghastly vision will be gone."

Argolicus probed. "Can you think of who would want to do this?"

"My brother," Marcus said. "Father is angry at him, as you saw, but he...he wouldn't do that to anyone. He is strict and blunt but not vengeful. In his own way, he cared about Lucas. Lucas was going off with no prospects. He wanted to support some crazy monk. He didn't want to become a cleric. He was looking at a life of poverty, at least the way he described it."

"And that's why your father is angry? Lucas chose a life outside the family tradition? A life that didn't bring honor to the family?"

"Yes. We would never see him again. Our family would be torn apart. Father believes we each have a responsibility to the family. Father wants the best for all of us." "By best, you mean wealth and power?" Marcus thought for a moment. "I hadn't looked at it that way... yes, wealth and power. Status.

We live comfortably. Giving up everything makes little sense. Lucas had so much to gain by staying with the family. It doesn't make sense to me and it certainly doesn't to Father."

"But from what I understand, Lucas was already at odds with your father. He had left to travel to Rome. It was happenstance, or fate, or the hand of God, as your father would call it, that he found this monk. Hadn't he already broken with your family?"

Marcus glanced at his brother's body, sprawled and rotting on the ground. "Yes. But we thought he would make a place for himself in the city. As the youngest son, he could gain influence for himself in some political role. Not everyone who meets a monk decides to follow his path."

"Just so," Argolicus said, thinking of Bartholomaeus' reason for cutting off his childhood friendship. He looked at Wiliarit standing among the flowers. His uncle gave him a knowing smile and nodded. "But, the monk is far away. Lucas was killed here. I don't see a connection."

Marcus shook his head, blinked his eyes, and stared again at his brother's body. "I hate to think this was purposeful. I mean against Lucas. I can't think of a reason for anyone to do this. Father and Lucas disagreed about almost everything. Mattheus took Father's side. His return home wasn't pleasant. But killing? Absolutely not. It must have been robbers who were angry he had nothing to steal. It doesn't make sense. To think someone deliberately killed Lucas... because he was Lucas, just doesn't make sense."

He shook his head again and motioned to the slaves. They brought a large blanket and spread it out next to Lucas' body. Four slaves gathered around the body and reached down to lift the body onto the blanket. Marcus counted down one, two, three. At the count of three, the slaves slid their hands under the body and began to lift it. The head wobbled backward and reddish fluid oozed out of the mouth and nose. One slave jumped back, almost losing hold of the body. Marcus signaled another slave to hold the head. The men lifted in unison and brought the body up off the ground. The right arm of the corpse flopped down. A slave reached out to place the arm on the torso. The skin on the hand slid down over the fingers.

Marcus cried out, once again, Argolicus wondered what the brother knew and whether he had killed Lucas. Whatever the reason, the killing was senseless.

Once the body was on the blanket, the slaves carried it off to the cart and covered it with another cloth. Marcus strode toward his horse nibbling on the fresh grass. But then, he turned around and came back to Argolicus who was helping Wiliarit fill the box of painting supplies.

"You were right to tell us. My father is abrupt and dogmatic. You always made Lucas enthusiastic when you two were young. I liked you for that."

"Lucas was my friend," Argolicus said as Marcus went to his horse, mounted, and followed the cart out of the meadow. He watched the horse thread its way from the meadow.

"Well," Wiliarit said, laying his vellum sheets in the box and closing the lid. "I see his father's imprint."

Argolicus watched his uncle lift the leather strap of the box to his shoulder. "Yes, of course. But he seemed genuinely distressed when he saw the body. He seems just as bewildered as we are." He searched in his folds for the scrap Maria had given him.

"What is it?" Nikolaos asked. "The sister. She said they were lying. I have it here somewhere." He fumbled through his tunic. "Aha," he said, pulling out the folded scrap. He read aloud from the note, "I will tell you the story of my brother. I will find you."

"That doesn't tell us much," Nikolaos said, shaking his head.

"You are best out of it. Stay away from that family. It will only open old wounds," Wiliarit said. He adjusted the strap of his painting box on his shoulder. "Let's go home. I, for one, could use some food." He patted his belly.

"He was my friend," Argolicus said as they all crossed the meadow to head toward the villa. The difference between his laughing, playful friend and the rotten corpse struck him. The gap of years was a blank. He knew little about Lucas. He thought about how he had changed in those years. His vision of himself at fifteen had been to follow in his father's foot-steps, grow into the estate, manage the property, and live comfortably. He hadn't envisioned years in Rome and the hard reality of the politics of powerful men.

"You haven't seen him for many years. Getting involved with that family was trouble then. It will be trouble now."

"These theological arguments, especially hating someone for their belief, or even their perceived belief from a narrow mind, make me angry. It's everywhere. People have arguments in the street in Rome. Men get into fights. It makes no sense. Where is the compassion?"

Wiliarit laid a hand on Argolicus shoulder. "You had two losses in quick succession. First, your father and, just when you needed friendship and kindness, you lost your friend. Those are wounds that leave scars."

"Do you think I am taking this too personally...mixing theological debates with my personal loss?"

"Only you can know. But, you could think about your personal involvement. This differs from being the supreme magistrate in Rome and resolving someone else's dilemma. Your memories and personal attachment, including how you feel about that family, may color your thinking."

"You are right. I'm best out of this. We've recognized his body, and the family has Lucas' body. There's no reason to be involved anymore." He smiled at Wiliarit. "I'll think about what you said. It's strange. You arrive and once again I'm mixed up with that family. Let's go home and let it rest." He turned to Nikolaos. "You'd think I'd remember all the old trails, but not just yet. Lead on."

Nikolaos led the way through the thick forest of trees. There wasn't a marked path, but he seemed to know the way. The warmth faded as they threaded through the trees. Argolicus followed, his mind lost in thoughts of his father, his friendship with Lucas, and the abrupt break that had shattered his youth. How had Lucas changed? He knew nothing about him as an adult. Wiliarit was probably right. He remembered a friend from childhood. Adult filters colored his memories. His recent life in Rome. filled with politics and a different corruption than an untended body, colored his memories.

"It's political," Wiliarit said. "It's the same in Constantinople. Theological differences and the Green and Blue Factions, fill the city with disagreements. I thought, at least here, I'd get away from all that and paint in peace."

"No," Argolicus said. "It's everywhere. The governor here spreads corruption and venal grasping rather than a steady hand on his reign. And, here the Church dominates and controls wealth and the landowners compete with the Church for power."

Wiliarit snorted. "The Church. But our Church came before. The Synod at Chalcedon was a political ploy orchestrated by the Emperor Constantine, not the bishops. Now here we are two centuries later where politics and religion walk hand in hand."

"In Rome, they say Ravenna is the most tolerant city in Italy. Theodoric has proclaimed religious tolerance and keeps those disturbances to a minimum."

"We're a long way from Ravenna. Your friend there, Cassiodorus, does he tell you this is true?" "He does, in his roundabout way." "As I said, we're a long way from Ravenna." "Yes, here tolerance is not a driving force. What makes trade go and who has more slaves these are the matters of concern. It's what people talk about. Look at Lucas' family. They're rich and intolerant."

"As in most places. I need to go to Ravenna and see for myself. I find it hard to believe one city would be so open to tolerance."

The trail opened to fields and they could see the villa and smoke coming from the kitchen chimney.

"Ah, food," Wiliarit exclaimed, smiling. "We're home." He picked up his pace and passed Nikolaos. The equipment in his paint box clacked against the wooden sides.

CHAPTER 3
FAMILY TREASURE

Three days later, Wiliarit labored at painting in Argolicus' study surrounded by his art supplies. He laid out a large sheet of vellum on an easel and drew the first lines of an illustration based on his sketches from his walks with Nikolaos. Even though the morning air was chilly, the door was open to let in more light.

Cries and clanking sounds rang from the far court where Argolicus and Nikolaos were at their daily fighting practices.

A shadow crossed Wiliarit's work at the same time he heard a female voice cry. "Oh!"

He turned to see a young woman covered in a red cloak.

"I... I thought," she stammered. "Where is Argolicus?"

"You're not mistaken. This is his study. I'm his uncle, Wiliarit, here on a visit. I'm afraid I've taken over his study."

"Wiliarit!," she exclaimed. "I've heard so much about you." Her forehead crinkled in perplexion as if he didn't fit her image. In her early twenties, she had an air of innocence like someone ten years younger.

"You have me at a disadvantage."

"I'm sorry, I was expecting Argolicus. I'm Maria. The sister of Lucas, the man he found in the meadow."

"Maria! I'm delighted. I'm so sorry about your brother. Let me take you to Argolicus although you could easily find him with all that clanging and shouting." He rose from his seat and joined her at the doorway. His plain monkish robe contrasted with her colorful red cloak as they headed toward the cries and clunks.

Maria smiled. "The action was what Lucas loved. Those

two were always doing something active as boys. Lucas used to tell me the wildest stories about shooting arrows from tree branches..."

Wiliarit launched one of his deep belly laughs. "Ah, the arrows. Did he tell you about wounding Julia's pet rabbit?"

"That, too. Argolicus brought out Lucas' adventuresome side." Maria's face changed, her brow wrinkling. "So sad about Julia."

"Ah, yes. Very sad." Wiliarit crossed himself. "Losing a wife and a son. I'm not sure he will replace her. Ah, here we are. The valiant swordsmen."

Argolicus raised his hand to Nikolaos to end their sparring.

Maria turned to Wiliarit. "Thank you. You are nothing like my father..." She paused. "You are nothing like I had imagined." She smiled at him and turned toward Argolicus.

"Maria," Argolicus said, putting down his sword. "Your note was mysterious. Are you here with answers?"

Wiliarit said, "I'm back to painting. Maria, it was a pleasure."

Maria smiled at him and turned to Argolicus. "It's not mysterious. My family..." She groped for words, looking down and then back up to Argolicus. "Lucas took what was his and caused a stir."

Argolicus raised an eyebrow. "What was his? That makes no sense. You need to start at the beginning for me to understand."

"I'm telling you this because Lucas trusted you. Because he trusted you, I trust you. But you must swear you won't tell anyone."

"No one. I'll keep your secret. But why tell me?" "Because you are the only one who can help. Father and my brothers are angry. They feel the sooner Lucas is buried and forgotten, they can forget the whole thing."

"The whole thing?" "I'm sorry. I'm not being clear. You are right. I'll start at the beginning."

"Good," Argolicus said as he dipped a cloth into a cistern and wiped his face.

"When each of us was born, Father commissioned an icon to celebrate the birth. He used the Greek iconographer in Rome, Calix. Did you hear of him when you were in Rome?"

Argolicus shook his head. "No. I thought iconographers do not sign their works."

"Yes, that's true," Maria said. "But he is known by word of mouth through his patrons. They are wealthy men like Father, and church dignitaries. Anyway, Lucas' icon is lovely, with a worked gilt background. Of course, it is the doctor and evangelist, Luke, his namesake. It is detailed with a winged ox, angels, and the dove descending from heaven."

"Oh, I'm sure Wiliarit would love to see it."

Maria smiled. "Wiliarit...he was painting when I discovered him in your study."

"Yes, but he creates books, not icons." "When we completed our formation and became members of the Church, Father had stands made for the icons. Not plain wood, but covered in gold leaf and inset with gems. Lucas took his."

"And that's what created the stir? Wouldn't he have a right to take his own icon?"

"That's where it gets complicated, and it involves other people."

"What other people?" "The bishop." They stood silently by the cistern. Argolicus felt the sun warm him through his thin exercise tunic. The bishop was a powerful man. He began to understand the complexity.

"The bishop kept the icons for safekeeping." "Yes, that's it exactly. When Lucas came back from Rome, he wanted the icon. He wanted to give it to that holy man he met, Benedictus. I'm not clear if he wanted to give it to Benedictus or sell it and give the proceeds to Benedictus. Lucas told us he would live with Benedictus. That, alone, was enough to make Father angry. But, the bishop was angry when he took the icon and the stand."

"The bishop was angry at Lucas, and your father was angry at him?"

Argolicus frowned. Lucas was straightforward and outspoken in his plain-speaking way. He understood how taking a family treasure, even though it theoretically belonged to him, would feel like a betrayal to a man like Bartholomaeus, headstrong and fervent in his religion.

"I'm not sure what happened because I learned most through Father's mutterings and rants. Lucas had left for the north. Father and Bishop Braga argued. Father believed he supported the bishop. The bishop felt the 'safeguarded' treasures were there for the Church. It boiled down to possession and power. Those are two areas where Father should not be crossed."

"And religion," Argolicus could not help saying as he remembered the childhood separation from his friend and his recent encounter with Bartholomaeus.

"Yes, religion. You certainly felt that hard edge. And that is why I am here."

"Why? I don't understand."

"Because someone killed my brother. I want to know who. Father feels Lucas betrayed the family by going outside religious tradition. That meant he went against Father's wishes. He's not a man of forgiveness. I don't want to think a family member killed him."

She paused, staring into the distance where the morning sun shone on the barn and the fields and rough hills beyond.

Argolicus didn't like Bartholomaeus or Maria's arrogant brothers. He felt his old friendship with Lucas welling inside with warm memories. He understood Lucas' desire to get away but didn't understand his new piety brought on by a visit to a hermit.

"Maria, I don't know how I can help you. I can't talk to your father or your brothers. They won't speak to me. I've always had warm feelings for Lucas, but I don't understand his recent turn to piety. Who is this Benedictus?"

"As much as I can tell from what Lucas said, he's a man against the false piety of the Church. I heard he even insulted a group of nearby monks who were supporting him. He believes in simple living and prayer. That's why I'm sure that Lucas was going to sell the icon in Rome and use the money to support his life with Benedictus. That's all I know."

"Whatever the reasons, Lucas decided to leave. I still can't help you. The other place to look would be the church and Bishop Braga, but I would be about as welcome there as at your father's. He would not welcome any questions from me about his feud with your father or what happened to the icon."

Maria sighed. Then she turned, put her arms around Argolicus, and hugged him. "Thank you for listening. I didn't know where to turn."

Then she pulled back and cried. "Lucas, Lucas," she murmured, "what were you thinking? Who did this to you?"

After she headed away on the path toward her home, Argolicus stood in the sunlight, frustrated that he couldn't help. He wanted to know the answer to his friend's murder.

❧

"And then she left." Argolicus sat in the courtyard garden with Nikolaos and Wiliarit. They were gathered around a breakfast table with bread, soft cheese, cooked eggs, and olives. Birds sang in the trees. The fountain his mother loved splashed in a soothing rhythm. He picked up his cup of honeyed milk.

"That poor girl," Nikolaos said, shaking his head. "She must look forward to her marriage."

"I'm sure she does," Argolicus said. "What a mixture of sorrow and freedom for a youngster. She was fond of Lucas."

Wiliarit broke off a big piece of bread from the round loaf, dipped it in wine, and chewed. Then he spoke. "I know how we can visit the bishop. I don't know how we can bring any conversation around to Lucas, but I know how to see the bishop."

"How?" Argolicus and Nikolaos asked in unison. "Pride and greed, They are great motivators." He leaned forward and pulled off another hunk of bread.

"Uncle, don't keep us in suspense. What's your idea?" "The patroness, Anica Juliana, will have her copy of Dioscorides soon. I'm here to finish up the last illustrations. Then I will look for a new project and a new patron. Surely a provincial bishop tucked away in a small town far away from emperors and princesses would want the services of a scribe with such well-known patrons... yes?"

"You would go to him and ask?"

"Well, he probably can't afford me, but I could arrange a time to speak with him. Religious differences like the nature of Christ are set aside when beautiful possessions enter the picture. I've seen it in Constantinople and Rome. I'm certain the same principles apply in Bruttia. Of course, you would accompany me as a local patrician." He leaned back, chewing on the wine-soaked bread, then plopped two olives into his mouth.

Argolicus slapped his hand on the table. "Now that's what I call a good idea."

Wiliarit picked up an egg and tapped the shell with his knife. "We would want a learned, articulate, and observant messenger to deliver my request," he said, looking at Nikolaos.

Nikolaos was up from the table. He ran to the study and returned with a sheet of vellum, a pen, and a pot of ink.

Wiliarit bit into the peeled, hard-cooked egg, causing half to disappear. "Most esteemed excellency, Your Grace, Braga, Bishop of Squillace," he began dictating. "Well, even if it's here in the hills and not the town of Squillace itself, he will eat it up."

Soon the letter was finished and Nikolaos was off to the bishop's palatial estate on the hill above the meadows.

"Naturally, I will ask to see his treasures so I can 'get a feeling for his excellent taste.' How else could I make a suggestion for the most appropriate book for his collection? Do you think he reads?" He helped himself to a second egg.

"I have no idea. Many clerics don't. He could be the exception, But, it doesn't matter. A beautiful book is a symbol of wealth." Argolicus answered. "Do I understand your plan? You will turn your conversation among the bishop's treasures to icons?"

"Aha, you understand," Wiliarit said, chuckling, as he broke off another piece of bread.

"Well, at least we will get his version of what happened with the icon and probably a few choice words about headstrong, misguided men like Lucas. I'm not convinced that will help us find the murderer, but it will shed light on a part of the story we don't know."

Argolicus decided an egg was a good choice. He was hungry after his morning bout with Nikolaos. He reached for the bowl of eggs and said, "Uncle, I don't know what I would have done without you. You are a family treasure."

The sun hid behind high clouds the next day as Wiliarit, Argolicus, and Nikolaos rode toward the bishop's palace. The horses pranced in the spring air, ready for a gambol. The men each kept a strong hand on the reins.

"Ah, what a smooth gait. Argolicus, you should ride more. No offense to Nikolaos, but riding will improve your skills just as much as all that pretend fighting you do."

Nikolaos kept silent. "A new stallion," said Argolicus. "He's particular about who he lets ride without resistance. I'll tell you the story about how we got him later. His name is Mercury's Flame, but we call him Flame."

Wiliarit patted the big red horse on the neck and whispered his name, "Flame." The stallion responded with a nod and a twist of his ears. "And look, all that sunshine yesterday opened more flowers. We're in luck, Nikolaos. I'll finish this book project in no time."

As they approached the palace, Argolicus saw movement everywhere. Slaves hurried around the palace grounds carrying equipment or working on building new structures. Children scurried carrying baskets. Crews of men worked on walls, pathways, and new buildings.

"More people than most towns," Argolicus said as he nodded toward the palace. "This new bishop has been busy while I was away in Rome."

"Aggressively so," Wiliarit said. "It's been longer than that since I looked up that hill."

"I was thinking of the letters of the Church Father Ignatius," Wiliarit said to Bishop Braga. "he advised, 'Follow the lead of your bishop.' Does that seem fitting?"

Bishop Braga stood eye to eye with Nikolaos but their height was the only similarity. Where Nikolaos was lithe, supple, and diminutive, Braga was broad and labored. His snub nose gave his face a child-like quality. He walked stiff-legged, like a dog approaching a fight. He wore his hair slicked with scented pomade above his round, smooth face. Although his clerical garments were plain wool, he wore several jeweled rings besides his bishop's ring. His elaborately worked, gold pectoral cross hung on a heavy gold chain. His voice was resonant with rounded vowels that would carry to the back of the nave.

"Would I be the only one to have this text?" the bishop asked.

"The only one in southern Italy," Wiliarit said. "Perhaps if you could show me your collection, I could get a better feel for how to produce the book and the most appropriate text to add to your library."

They were gathered in the *salutorium*, grand presence room, a large, empty, wide room barren of furniture except for the bishop's ornately carved chair. Three deacons stood in silence behind the bishop dressed in similar clerical dark woolen robes.

Argolicus watched the round bishop puff with pride even though the bishop's words told a different story.

"Well, you must realize," he nodded at Wiliarit, "that this is nothing like you see in Constantinople or Rome." He looked at Argolicus, "Your Excellency, I hope, with friends like Boethius, you will not disparage our humble cumulation, but you will see what we have is quite excellent. The Church cannot survive without support. We are the guardians of local wealth. The wealth supports the Church."

Argolicus realized the bishop knew more about him than they had intended for this visit. He decided to speak as little as possible and let Wiliarit lead while he observed. He knew Nikolaos, silent in this situation, would also watch everything. They could compare insights once they returned home.

Braga led them out of the *salutorium* with his stiff-legged walk into a long hallway where slaves bustled on errands. Outside, they followed a long portico whose arches looked out onto a vast courtyard garden filled with shrubs and herbs. The sun broke through the clouds sending rays streaming light into the garden greenery, shimmering on the leaves. At the end of the covered walkway, they came to a large warehouse with a transverse bar that slid in a groove carved into the floor in front of the door. Braga signaled to the slaves guarding the entrance. They stooped to unlock the pin that held the great locking beam in place and slid the beam along its course groove on the stone floor to bar the door."

In here," Braga said, "we store goods for safekeeping." He led them into the warehouse filled with boxes of all sizes and floor to ceiling shelving where luxury items lay side by side in no seeming order. Gold glittered on uncovered items while several shelves were arrayed with icons of saints with gilt halos, some with entire backgrounds of gold. Another shelf contained goblets of gold and silver, many set with large glittering stones or pearls. In one corner, heaps of swords and daggers leaned against the wall.

Three slave women worked among the treasures, brushing away dust and wiping surfaces with soft cloths. Their chatter ceased as the group entered.

"The Church cannot survive without support. We are the guardians of local wealth. The wealth supports the Church, the Church supports the land. Mico," he said, turning to a deacon, "Open the treasure room."

The deacon was much taller than the bishop. Underneath his plain robe, his body emanated power in contrast to the bishop's posturing. His dark brown eyes fastened on Wiliarit and, then, Argolicus before he turned to the door. He unclasped a large lock and opened the door into another room.

"We hold our supporters' personal treasures here," Braga said as he led them all into the room. "They add to our resources."

"I'm getting a sense of your preferences," Wiliarit said, gazing around the array, his eyes taking stock of the goods.

The bishop looked up at the large scribe. A flicker of a grimace crossed his face before he composed his expression into a smile. "Oh, no, these are not my personal preferences. These are goods given to the Church for safekeeping. They reflect the tastes of their owners."

Argolicus held his tongue when he heard the word given. Braga had a way of distorting his language to make it appear the goods here were his.

Wiliarit nodded and then asked, "So these beautiful items," he waved his massive arm to encompass everything in the present room and in the room they had just left, "are given to the Church. Such a tribute to your spiritual leadership."

"Oh. we do have donations," Braga tried to look humble. "In that room," he said, pointing to the first room, "are goods donated to the Church. Some are bequests of deceased members and some are given in true generosity by our fold. As I said, without the support of our patrons the Church would not flourish." His chest expanded, almost reaching the expanse of his middle girth.

"And this room?" Wiliarit questioned. "What about the goods in this room?"

"Well," Braga said with hesitation. "These are here for safekeeping."

"Safekeeping?" Wiliarit echoed Argolicus' thought.

"Yes, safekeeping. In Bruttia, we have so much unrest. At times, the unrest surges into violence. You may not have heard of the local bishop who was murdered several years ago." He glanced at Argolicus. "In the North, the King's peace reigns. Here, far from Ravenna and the heretic king, the people are dissatisfied. Venantius, our governor, is more interested in acquiring wealth than governing. So we must take care of ourselves. Patrons of the Church send us articles, which we may use while they are here, for safekeeping in our secure warehouse. For instance, our closest neighbor and largest patron, Bartholomaeus, has many items here. As a wealthy landowner, he feels vulnerable to the local unrest."

"Yes, I know of him," Wiliarit said. "his son was brutally murdered while out in the countryside. I'm sure you heard about it. I was the one who discovered his body. Gruesome."

"Bartholomaeus was here. He told me about his son's murder. And the discovery." He flashed a look at Argolicus.

Argolicus knew the bishop was well aware of who he was and his religious heritage. The bishop was wily, not saying anything, but conveying that he knew at least part of their ruse. But, that would not keep them from exploring what was here at the bishop's palace.

"Ah, Lucas," Braga said. "A young man who strayed from the Church. He was here recently. He's... he was quite the brash man. Imagine! He tried to tell us we, the Church, should let go of material things and lead people in the spirit of Christ."

"In the spirit of Christ?" Wiliarit asked. "Do you mean like Peter?"

"Yes, exactly like Peter in the Acts of the Apostles. To give up everything. We have our Tradition. Tradition keeps the body of the Church together, leading people to participate in sound ways. Without support of physical goods, the Church would flounder."

Wiliarit nodded. Bishop Braga continued, "He pestered me with his talk. I gave him to Mico to claim his icon and be gone."

"Yes, Your Grace. He found the icon, wrapped it in cloth, and left." The deacon gestured toward a shelf of icons.

"So, these items in safekeeping belong to their owners, are kept here to be safe, but are accessible at any time to their owners?" Wiliarit asked.

"Exactly," Braga answered. "It's an arrangement for mutual protection. Should either our church buildings here or the landowner's villas come under threat, we support each other with men and arms. I'm sure you saw some of our weapons in the other room."

Wiliarit continued, "So, when that young man Lucas came here to retrieve an icon, there was no problem?"

"No, no, no. The goods are here. Mico or another deacon unlocks the warehouse and oversees the removal. We want to make sure no other goods are taken that belong to other patrons."

"Ah," Wiliarit said. "That makes sense." Argolicus nodded agreement, thinking of the ways avaricious men took any opportunity to gain more, more of anything that would add to their personal riches.

Wiliarit asked, "And the icon was all that Lucas wanted?"

"Your Grace, with your permission," the deacon Mico said. Braga nodded his head. "He, Lucas, the young man... he wanted just the icon. But you have to understand that we were reluctant. Although he was like his father—committed, fevered. For him, everything was black and white. To combat his father's fervor, he found his own. He was against the Church and our traditions. Our Church, the Church that leads the community here. I tried to persuade him to leave the icon here, or at least wait until we consulted with his father, Bartholomaeus. But no, he wanted the icon. He said it was his birthright. He wanted to... it was a garbled story... give it to some man near Rome. Not a priest, not a monk, just a man who lives in a cave. He took it, wrapped it in linen, and placed it in a cloth carrying bag."

"Interesting," Wiliarit said. "In my travels, I've encountered many interpretations of Church and property. This thinking of Lucas harkens back to the beginnings. But the Church has grown since then."

Braga and the deacon, Mico, nodded. "Indeed," Braga said. "I was glad to see him go. We have enough trouble here with displaced farmers and the like always asking for more. More support. More work. It's impossible to give to everyone. I've talked with Bartholomaeus about this. It's the landowners' place," he glanced at Argolicus again, "to keep the people in check."

Argolicus crossed his arms over his chest, using a physical action to keep himself from speaking. This bishop—young, power hungry, and determined to remain in charge—did his utmost to keep his wealthy followers under his wing. Wiliarit interrupted his thoughts.

"But, let's look at some of the items. Your Grace, show me which are your favorites. That will help me determine if Ignatius would be an apt selection for you. You are still interested, yes?"

"Oh, yes," Braga said. "Let me show you the icons. My books are scant."

CHAPTER 5
STRATEGY WITHOUT A PLAN

"I can't stop thinking how lonely Lucas must have been," Argolicus said.

In the study, Argolicus reviewed what had happened in the last few days. Even though Bartholomaeus had separated him from his friend, he should have kept track. He had learned that friends in life were rare. Why hadn't he paid more attention to Lucas? And when Lucas left home and went to Rome, somehow, he should have known and renewed their friendship. He himself had been in Rome. How had their disconnection remained so strong? How much of it was due to his own neglect?

Wiliarit sat dabbing with his paints at a rendering of a bramble. Nikolaos read Herodotus, getting ready for the next oral reading this evening.

"Lonely and disturbed," Wiliarit said not looking up from his twining bramble, his brush dabbing a dark green at emerging leaves.

"Yes, I feel that somehow I should have..."

"No," Wiliarit said. "Everyone knew you were in Rome. He could just as easily have reached out to you. He didn't. None of this is your fault." He dipped his brush in a cup of water, wiped it clean with a cloth, and laid it down on the table. "Better to concentrate on helping Maria if you want to be soft on someone. There's no going back to change actions. Who do you think killed that lonely, disgruntled man?"

"From what I understand, he didn't feel disgruntled. He was on a path of truth. His truth, but a truth. It's that truth of his that made others disgruntled."

Nikolaos put down the history book. "I hear about that Benedictus. Slaves talk about him. There are rumors. The strongest one is that he insulted a group of monks who reached out to him. I'm not sure about the details. You know how rumors are."

Argolicus nodded. He knew about the distortions of rumors.

"This Benedictus must be an Italian rumor because I haven't heard a word about him in Constantinople," Wiliarit said. "But the western Church and the eastern Church are at odds so rumors may not transfer."

Argolicus nodded. "Ah, the Emperor Zeno stirred up a hornet's nest. I think the Acacian division may be with us for a while. Clerics are so touchy about these theological points."

"Precisely," Wiliarit said. "So the ultra-conservative Bishop Braga would staunchly oppose anything that went against his Church, especially some discontented man like Lucas who came with messages counter to tradition. I can tell you right now he would not approve of the Henotikon or any attempts to include 'heretics' in the Church. Of course, that includes us. Our tradition is older than his, but his is the prevailing one here in southern Italy."

"Greed was the main reason he saw us today. You were so right to play to his vanity, Uncle. If we discover who killed Lucas, the family may have to plead to our governor, Venantius. He is just as prideful and greedy. Depending on who killed Lucas, the final decision may come down to who pays the governor the greater fee."

"But, that's the question," Nikolaos said. "Who killed Lucas? Maybe it wasn't about his errant belief but for some other reason."

Argolicus reached behind Wiliarit and pulled a vellum sheet from a stack. "Who do we know so far that had a reason?"

"The father," Nikolaos said. "What an angry man."

Argolicus wrote Bartholomaeus at the top of the sheet. "Yes, his son had disobeyed him. But, what reason would he have to kill him? He is powerful enough to deliver that blow." He scribbled some notes next to the father's name. "But his brother Mattheus is just as strong." He wrote Mattheus. "And he's actually more irrational than Bartholomaeus. The father has an iron will but Mattheus seems to fly off the handle, mainly to impress his father. What a tortured father and son relationship."

"Haven't you found that it's often the quiet ones?" Wiliarit said. "What about the brother Marcus? He was the most conciliatory when we announced finding Lucas. After all, he came to retrieve the body while the father stewed in anger. But that could be a show. Maybe he made that show to cover up his guilt."

Argolicus wrote Marcus. "Perhaps. But, he seems easily swayed without conviction. I don't see him getting angry enough, but you are right. It is often the quiet ones."

They sat in silence for a moment each trying to decipher who would kill Lucas. Then Argolicus picked up his pen and wrote Braga.

"The bishop had motive," he said. "I don't see him physically confronting Lucas. But he has numerous slaves. I'm sure he has a coterie of thugs for enforcement. He has to manage those hundreds of slaves. And from what I gathered from our visit to the bishop, he wields power with the patricians as well. He could have set one or more out to follow and waylay Lucas after he left the palace."

"One supposed heretic?" Nikolaos said. "That doesn't seem worth the risk for a man with so much power. Why would he risk his reputation and all of his worldly goods for one recreant? Lucas didn't have any political power, like his father. Essentially he had been thrown out of the family."

"Nikolaos, you've seen the street brawls in Rome over religious fervor. It doesn't take much to get someone fired up," Argolicus said. "But you are right. The bishop would have little motive to kill a recreant. It would be better to let him leave and never return."

"Yes, Master, but those rioters are street people. I don't see the bishop risking his reputation and position for one person who will soon be gone."

"Maybe he was in collusion with Bartholomaeus. The bishop had the thugs at hand. Bartholomaeus needed men for hire. I'm considering possibilities." He scribbled on the vellum sheet.

"Are you forgetting, Maria?" Wiliarit asked. "Talk about quiet ones."

"I understand your 'quiet ones' but I don't see her instigating murder. I mean, why? She's the one that risked coming here to ask us for help."

They all sat in silence again. Argolicus stared at the vellum sheet hoping some new thought would come.

Hoofbeats clattered in the courtyard. In minutes, Argolicus' friend, Ebrimuth, found his way to the study door. Every inch of his tall frame declared his heritage from The People — broad shoulders, thick light-blond hair flowed down his back, a dagger strapped to his side over a richly embroidered tunic.

"I knew I'd find you here."

"Ebrimuth, you remember my uncle, Wiliarit."

"The Father and the Son," Ebrimuth said, filling the doorway with his energetic frame.

"Worship and glorify," answered Wiliarit. "I think we've gathered The People of this area in one place," Argolicus said laughing.

"Oh, no," Ebrimuth answered. "I have a household full of

Our People. Hasn't your mother told you?" He gave Argolicus an arch look with his light blue eyes.

"My mother may hear things, but we don't gossip," Argolicus said.

"Well, I'm here with gossip...news," Ebrimuth said, shoving his broad shoulders through the door as Nikolaos pulled up a chair for him to sit.

"And?" Argolicus said smiling. Somehow Ebrimuth and his boundless energy always made him feel invigorated as if the energy transferred from one body to another.

"Your friend Lucas. Everyone is speculating on what could have happened."

"That's what we were doing," Argolicus said, holding up the vellum sheet. "Do you have any thoughts?"

"I do," Ebrimuth said, settling his vibrant body into the chair. "And I don't. Everyone was wondering where Lucas stayed when he was here. He obviously couldn't stay with his family. He came to me."

Argolicus felt the sting of not helping again. "What? With you?"

"He didn't want to cause problems for you. He knew how much his father disliked you...us...Our People. He wanted to retrieve his icon and then go back to Rome. His father told him to never set foot in the house. He was here only a few days. No one would think of looking for him at my house."

"Well, you are right about that," Argolicus said. "It didn't occur to me. I thought he was staying at an inn."

"He wanted safety and a place to be inconspicuous. He felt an inn was too public."

"It worked. No one knew where he was. But what did you think when he disappeared?" Argolicus asked.

Ebrimuth shifted his large shoulders and shook his head of long blonde hair. "I didn't think much except I thought it was strange he hadn't said farewell. He left in the morning for the bishop's palace and I never saw him again. He didn't say much while he stayed. A bit about his father and his brothers turning against him. It seemed to strengthen his resolve to leave for good. I should have come to you when I noticed he left his travel bag."

"He left for the bishop's palace to get the icon?"

"Yes."

"We visited the bishop. Lucas left with the icon. Not on good terms, but he left. That seems to be the last time anyone saw him. What was in the travel bag?"

"I brought it with me," Ebrimuth said. He pulled a leather strap on his shoulder and removed the satchel. He opened it up and looked at Argolicus. "He's dead now. It won't matter if we look." He pulled his chair closer to the table, upended the bag, and emptied the contents onto the table.

Wiliarit and Nikolaos drew up to the table as Ebrimuth's large hand spread out the contents. Leggings, underwear, two tunics. A book. Nothing.

"No papers. Nothing that helps us find a murderer," Argolicus said as the others pulled back. "Are you sure he said nothing that might help?"

"He wasn't chatty. Twice he said, 'I'm done with Bruttia.' That's it."

Argolicus picked up the vellum sheet and stared. "His father out of pride. His older brother. The bishop."

"Maybe it was a robbery gone wrong," Nikolaos said. "He was fighting for his life and a robber hit him."

"Maybe. But look at those clothes. Was he dressed more formally when he left for the bishop's palace? Did he look rich?" Argolicus said.

"No," Ebrimuth said. "His clothing was indistinguishable from what you see there."

"I'm missing something. Something important. I feel like

it's right in front of me but I'm not seeing it." Argolicus slapped down the vellum sheet.

"I could get one of my men to ask around. See if there's any news about somebody suddenly rich, or who left. Nikolaos could do the same thing. Ask questions where we would get no answers."

"I could do that," Nikolaos said. "It's worked in the past."

Ebrimuth started putting the clothing back in the satchel. "This belongs to his family now. Do you think they want it?"

"Unlikely," Argolicus said. "But that reminds me. I need to send a note to Maria. Just a quick one telling her I've found nothing. We could give the contents to her. She may want to give these things to a slave."

"I'm off then," Ebrimuth said. He stood up, patted Argolicus on the shoulder, and strode out the door.

"Such energy," Wiliarit said, nodding toward the empty doorway.

Argolicus smiled. "He's a doer not a thinker. He must have been uncomfortable with Lucas' brooding. Such opposites. But, then Lucas found a solution to his problem. Hidden in plain sight." He turned to Nikolaos. "I'll write a note to Maria. You can take it and this satchel. Then spend some time with servants and slaves. See if you can learn anything."

Argolicus scribbled on another sheet of vellum, folded it, and handed it to Nikolaos.

Wiliarit stirred a pot of paint and dipped in a brush. "I'm thinking about the Church. Braga is more than one man insatiable for ownership. He is the Church."

Outside a new set of hooves clattered in the courtyard. Argolicus stood. "It seems to be a day for visitors."

A young slave girl knocked at the entrance to the study. "Your mother wants you in the atrium."

The elder brother Mattheus' embroidered shoes slapped the marble floor as he paced. He stopped when Argolicus entered the atrium, balancing his bulk with widespread feet.

"I'll leave you to talk," Amalina, Argolicus' mother, said. Her light blue tunic reflected the light in her eyes. Her long braid swished against her back and the dagger scabbard hanging from her waist shifted against her thigh as she walked toward the kitchen.

"Mattheus," Argolicus said. "Welcome. Have you found out something about Lucas?"

Mattheus ignored his question. "I thought my father was clear. Stay out of our family business. We already asked you and the next thing I hear you've been visiting the bishop, asking questions." He brought his bulky frame up close to Argolicus. "Stay away."

Argolicus kept his anger in check and expressed his first thought. "Is this you speaking your father's words?"

"It doesn't matter who says the words. They are clear enough. Stay away." Mattheus crossed his arms over his silk tunic.

Argolicus kept silent looking the posturing man in the eye.

"Yes, my father sent me," Mattheus finally continued. He dropped his arms and balled his fists. "He can't stand the thought of you. This is a family matter. You are no part of our family. Stay away. Don't get involved."

Argolicus thought about telling him about the nature of

the visit, Wiliarit and the book, but he knew it would be useless. And, in a sense, he was right. And, if word had come to Bartholomaeus, then something was off because the visit was about creating a book. They had created a reason to visit the bishop, but it was all the bishop knew. He hedged.

"I can't feed your fears. The visit was about another matter, not Lucas. If I see the bishop, or the wine merchant, or the horse breeder, that is my concern." He was finding his anger was pushing at him. He could feel his face getting red.

"But my father heard..." Mattheus spluttered and then grew silent.

"Rumors are not truth. You stay out of my matters. I'll stay out of yours. Tell your father that is my agreement."

Mattheus lost his bluster. "I will." He turned and shuffled across the marble, his silks rustling in empty bravado. Then he stopped and turned. "Why? Why do you care about Lucas' murder?"

"He was my friend. I cared about him. I'm baffled why he didn't get in touch with me if he was having serious trouble."

"He wasn't having 'serious trouble' that I know. Of course, Father was angry at him and his crazy plan to go follow a monk in a cave. If you were a father wouldn't that give you concern?"

Argolicus hadn't seen it that way before. His own prejudice and lingering resentment stood in his way. He considered the new perspective. "I was thinking of Lucas' right to make his own decisions. You are right, I would have questions about the wisdom of such a major decision."

"He was my brother. I thought he was doing it out of spite. I can't imagine a rational man giving up everything. His status. It was the rest of his life." Mattheus pulled his forehead together in a frown. "It's unthinkable."

"Religious callings puzzle those who don't experience them," Argolicus said. "I don't understand, and, yet, my uncle, was called to be a monk. It doesn't make him less of a person. Just different. He is quite pleasant company."

"Yes, but he's not part of the Church. That's why Father wanted Lucas away from him long ago. Do you think Lucas was rebelling against..."

"No, I don't think that. Lucas was wiser than to bear out a grudge against your father for something that happened long ago. If he was following a monk, it was because that monk spoke to him, not because your father forbade meeting with Wiliarit years ago. Our Church, the King, Theodoric, and all of us of the People follow a Christian tradition that is older than your present Trinitarian theology. Lucas wasn't a student of theology. That is different from a man of faith."

"I'm not prepared to discuss theology. Think of me as a man a faith, one different from yours. I came to deliver my father's message." Mattheus started to turn and then said, "I remember how Lucas enjoyed your company. You two had fun, from what I can tell. I'm not sure I ever had fun."

He startled Argolicus. "You didn't play as a child?"

"A different kind of play—board games, puzzles. But I didn't have a friend to romp through the woods, climb trees. I didn't have adventures like the two of you. As the eldest, Father expected me to set an example for the others. My example was the Church. My example is the Church. I think Lucas was impetuous and foolish to leave our family." Mattheus crossed his arms over his chest and dipped his chin. "With his new turn, I'm not certain he would consider me his friend."

Argolicus tried to imagine giving up his life to live in a cave. He couldn't. "But, regarding your father, I see no reason for us to cross paths."

Mattheus lifted his hands in a placating gesture, turned and left the atrium.

Argolicus walked the passage to the *peristylum* lost in

thought. Lucas hadn't come to see him on his return. From a rational point of view he could understand how he didn't want to stir up old troubles with his father. But even after he'd had a row with his father he went to Ebrimuth. Not a word to his old friend. Not even a note. He felt slighted.

Was he good at friendship? He'd known Ebrimuth since childhood and would trust his life with his wild friend. But, all the time he'd been in Rome and known people, even worked at meeting people, he'd not had a friend. Not someone he could spend time with in a casual way or share his thoughts. Maybe that was why he was so upset with Lucas' murder. He stopped pacing and sat down on a bench in front of the fountain.

He was taking this murder personally. With all the crimes and murders he had investigated in Rome it was a matter of getting to the root of the problem. This time he felt the loss. He thought about all the family members and friends he'd spoken with who had been feeling loss and bewilderment.

"There you are," Wiliarit said, approaching from the kitchen with a bowl of radishes. "Want a radish? I think this is the best time of year for radishes, juicy and tart." He held out the bowl.

Argolicus took a large, red radish, trimmed and scrubbed clean, and bit in. He watched the fountain water play in the light of the open room.

"Lost in thought?" Wiliarit asked as he sat on the bench beside Argolicus.

"Mmmm," Argolicus mumbled, chewing.

"The brother. What did he want?"

"He was his father's messenger. Stay out of our family affairs. Somehow they knew we'd been to visit the bishop. News travels quickly. Of course, I couldn't tell him his own sister had asked us to look into Lucas' death. But that wasn't what I was thinking about."

"What, then?"

"Friendship. How precious it is. Especially for me. I don't have many friends. Knowing many people and having friends are two different things. Even though I hadn't seen Lucas in years, his death touched me. I thought I was inured to death and murder, but when it happens to a friend, I can't help but feel a loss."

Wiliarit stared at the one large radish left in the bowl. "You feel a personal responsibility to find the killer. Not just because Maria asked for help."

"Yes. I can't seem to separate her request from my personal interest. And... I'm angry. Angry at Lucas for not reaching out to me."

"That's the hard part, not being able to control other people's actions. I have my faith when I am disappointed. What do you have?" Wiliarit took the last radish, popped it in his mouth, and crunched in satisfaction.

"That's just it. I think of myself as rational, especially when investigating a murder. But feelings keep creeping in. I feel slighted because Lucas didn't contact me. He stayed with Ebrimuth and never said a word to me. I have sympathy for Maria. Not just that her brother was murdered, but that Bartholomaeus is so overbearing. And, then, how can I help her if I'm not rational?"

"Here's what I've learned, if you don't mind advice from an old man."

"No, no. Tell me."

"When emotions start to knock you off kilter, keep doing what you are doing. Just the physical activity helps to put everything back in perspective."

Argolicus nodded. "And, find a wife. A good woman helps keep you balanced."

Argolicus chortled. "Now you sound like Mother."

"Are you talking about me?" Amalina entered the *peri-*

stylum from the direction of the kitchen. She crossed the marble floor with a grace most middle-aged women had lost years before.

"Mother, you'll be happy to hear that Uncle Wiliarit has suggested I find a wife."

She raised an eyebrow at Wiliarit.

"Amalina, you know how we all respect your wisdom."

"I know something is up when my brother tries to flatter me. What are you two plotting?"

"Mother, it's nothing. Uncle was consoling me... in his way. It's just that I'm surprised at how Lucas' murder is affecting me."

"Not by that insufferable man who was just here?"

"No. I think he's even more lost than I am. His father rules his life. I'm not sure he has an original thought or would recognize one if he had it. He's like most bullies. Empty inside. I'm upset about Lucas."

"Lucas was a childhood friend. Of course, it upset you," Amalina said as she crinkled her brow in sympathy.

"It's not that. I feel as though the friendship didn't mean that much to him. He stayed with Ebrimuth and I didn't even know he was here."

"Ebrimuth explained why," Wiliarit said. "I think you may be frustrated that you can't find his killer."

"Maybe." Argolicus frowned. Was his mind so untrustworthy? He had been fond of Lucas. They had been best friends when they were young. "Maybe, I'm mourning my youth."

Amalina said, "Maybe, the best act of friendship you can do now is to find his killer."

Argolicus smiled. "Mother, you are always right... except when you talk about marriage."

All three of them laughed.

"That's for another day," Wiliarit said. "Let's get back to

thinking about the possible killers. We didn't add bandits or robbers to your list."

"I'm off to talk to the overseer, Amalina said. "Hand me that bowl. I'll send it to the kitchen." She turned to look at Argolicus. "You could help me with running the estate. When was the last time you talked with Lucius? No, don't answer. I know it's been awhile. You could add that to your schedule along with fighting and reading."

Wiliarit gave her the empty radish bowl. Amalina walked toward the kitchen, her long, blonde braid swaying down her back. Argolicus mentally added managing the estate, at least talks with Lucius, the overseer, to his daily activities. Then his mind returned to the murder.

"Bandits seem unlikely. Except for the fact that Lucas was alone, he wasn't a likely robbery target. He was wearing a linen tunic, but nothing, except the ring, made him a likely target and the ring was still on his finger. No, it was someone with a different motive."

"Well, the icon is missing. From what the deacon said it was in a modest cloth sack. Hardly an item to catch a bandit's eye. You're probably right. What about that brother that was just here?"

"If anything, his actions convinced me that he is just a shell. He doesn't have the spirit to kill so brutally. We can't rule him out, but he is empty inside. Conniving, possibly, but brutal, no."

Argolicus watched the sunlight playing in the flow of water in the fountain.

"Master," Nikolaos said, rushing into the open space. "I delivered the note, but there is a complication. Everything is chaotic at Bartholomaeus house. Maria was in tears. I could hear Bartholomaeus arguing with Mattheus. This murder has caused confusion in that house."

Argolicus looked up. "I just told Mattheus I would stay

out of their family's affairs. But we will keep looking for the murderer."

"You will have an uncomfortable conversation, then," Nikolaos said. "Maria is on her way."

"This will be tense," Wiliarit said. "I'm going to find some fortification for us all." He headed toward the kitchen.

CHAPTER 7
THE MARIA QUANDARY

"Ah," Wiliarit said as a slave brought a tray with eggs, honey vinegar pine nut sauce, and a small pitcher of garum and laid it out on a table in the peristylum.

"You see, we can meet here." He took an egg from the bowl, dipped it in the sauce, and poured on a drop of garum. "Just what I needed."

A second slave arrived with the paint box and a board. "I can paint here in the light," Wiliarit said, producing a vellum sheet and attaching it to the board. He settled in on the bench next to Argolicus as the slaves arranged his painting equipment.

Argolicus ignored the food as he listened to Nikolaos reporting on his delivery.

"You could hear Bartholomaeus arguing with Braga, the bishop. Not the words, just the argument. I went in by the slave entrance. A slave took your note to Maria."

"Why was Braga there? It must be important for him to leave his palace and go to Bartholomaeus," Argolicus said.

"I don't know. Their voices were harsh. The father is very loud. As I said, I couldn't hear the words, just the loud voices."

The afternoon sunlight slanted on the water fountain.

"Borage," Wiliarit said. "Just the right herb to add to the sauce. Delightful. Amalina knows how to keep a good kitchen. Try one."

Argolicus took an egg, dipped it in the honeyed sauce, and poured out a drop of garum. He bit into the tasty concoction and turned his head as a slave entered the peristylum followed by Maria. She entered the sunlight and crossed the marble floor.

"I came as soon as I could," Maria said. "Lucas taught me all the trails and even the ways here that have no trails." She smiled.

"Maria," Wiliarit said. "Sit down, sit down. Have an egg."

Maria came over and sat down next to Argolicus, ignoring the eggs. She threw back the folds of her red cloak. "Ah, the sun. A warm March day. Who could believe all these troubles on such a lovely day? But, I am here about trouble."

She turned to Argolicus who asked, "There's more trouble? Lucas' death isn't enough?"

"I'm afraid. Father is angry. He seems to be angry at everyone and everything. He had a huge argument with Mattheus when he came back from seeing you. Father hit him. Marcus tried calming him down. He can usually get Father to calm down, but not today. I thought he would hit Marcus, too. But, he retreated just in time. Then Bishop Braga came. I don't know why. Ordinarily, Father goes to the palace. Their shouts echo throughout the house. Father is terrifying when he goes into a rage." She took in a deep breath. Her large eyes widened. "I'm afraid. I don't know what to do."

Argolicus remembered how Bartholomaeus had threatened Lucas and kept him in a room for days. How just when he needed a friend after his father's death, his best friend had been locked away and threatened with beatings. The rage Bartholomaeus had poured out on Wiliarit who was with his sister in her grief. It had been a defining moment. He had questioned Christianity, and the questions had never left.

Maria interrupted his thoughts. "I want to be somewhere else until the wedding. It's just weeks away. Father has suggested I put it off for a year of mourning. I can't live there. I can't stand it. Living in fear, afraid to say anything about

Lucas while my heart is breaking at his death. When Father goes into a rage, it can last for days. I'm terrified he will try to delay the wedding. It's like a dark cloud in our house." She closed her eyes to stop tears, but they rolled down her cheeks.

Nikolaos slipped away into the house.

"And, and," she continued, "thank you for your note. I shouldn't have asked for your help. It complicated everything. The bishop is angry. My father is angry. Lucas was honest. I'm sorry I preyed on your old friendship. How could one honest man cause so much turmoil? Do you think my father could have done this? Or sent a slave to do it? Should I be afraid of my father? I mean really afraid?" The tears kept rolling down, and she started sobbing.

Wiliarit sat as if in contemplation, but Argolicus knew his uncle's mind was churning with ideas.

Argolicus said, "Didn't your mother have a sister? Don't you have cousins? Can you stay with them until your father calms down?"

Nikolaos came back into the garden and handed Maria a linen cloth. She took the cloth, wiped her cheeks and sniffling nose and then shook her head.

"They moved north. That was soon after your father died. There is no one." She subsided into tears again.

Argolicus felt trapped. He wanted to help her but already felt his alliance with this family had caused too much trouble.

They all sat quietly in the March sun each with their own thoughts.

"I came as soon as I could," Amalina said rushing out from the kitchen area with a cup in her hand. "Nikolaos told me Maria was here." She sat down on the bench next to Maria and put her arm around the young woman's shoulder. "Here, drink some of this tea."

Maria wiped her face again, looked up, and took the cup.

She sipped the cup. And sipped again. "This is good. Thank you."

"Why don't you come inside with me," Amalina said as she took the cup from Maria. "You can drink the tea and I'll give you a snack. You'll feel better."

Maria nodded. Amalina guided her out of the peristylum into the back of the house.

"Well," said Wiliarit, dabbing green onto an outlined leaf on his board. "What a quandary. She comes to the one place that will infuriate her father the most. The two of us being unacceptable heretics." He reached out and patted Argolicus' shoulder.

Argolicus shook his head. "I feel for her, but we can't get involved at that personal level. I told her I would look into Lucas' murder, but then today I told Mattheus that I would stay out of their family business. I've put myself in a box and don't know how to get out."

He took an egg and dipped it in the sauce. "I think I'm eating more since your arrival." He patted his stomach.

"Food is a solace," Wiliarit said, reaching for another egg. "Especially in worrisome times. Let's see if we can solve the murder and rid you of your burden. What about the other brother, Marcus?" He plopped the rest of the egg in his mouth, wiped his fingers, and began dabbing tiny yellow dots in the center of a white flower.

"Unless he did it at his father's bidding. It's hard to tell," Argolicus answered. "It's hard to tell about any of them. Maybe the father, given to rage, hired thugs."

"None of them look guilty," Wiliarit said applying yellow dots to another white flower. Nikolaos moved behind him to watch him work.

"You've traveled to cultured places like Constantinople, Burgundia, and even Rome, but in the role of a bookmaker. From a monk's perspective people reveal their shortcomings in the eyes of God. But, as a magistrate, I've found that people hide their feelings and especially their motivations. The innocent can appear guilty and the guilty act reverent and beyond reproach."

Wiliarit nodded his head as he concentrated on the center of another flower on the vellum.

"And, how can we really know people?" Argolicus continued. "My feelings for Lucas are based on a boy I knew over fifteen years ago. Who knows how he matured, or even if he matured? Remember how he was a daredevil, hanging from tree branches, and riding horses at full gallop over fields riddled with rodent holes. He took risks without thinking."

Wiliarit nodded again. "We don't know what he said or did to other people when he came back from the North. He could have angered one of his brothers about something other than going to live with the monk. He could have offended anyone. We don't know who he saw or what he did."

"Those look so lifelike," Nikolaos said, peering over Wiliarit's shoulder.

"Thanks to you showing me where to find those spring flowers. Do you have any thoughts about Lucas?"

Nikolaos was quiet for a moment. "I agree with Argolicus. We don't know how he acted as an adult. We don't know enough."

Wiliarit went back to the leaves with a different green. "Yes, as a monk I devote my life to God. I have made my choice. I can understand how Lucas could make a similar decision. My interaction with Bartholomaeus years ago was painful and from what you say his temper and strict beliefs have not softened over the years. But, I am also wondering how he could have angered Braga."

"I'm listening," Argolicus said. Bartholomaeus' clash with Wiliarit and the end of his friendship with Lucas was tied in his mind with his father's death.

"Clerics have a different focus than, say, a monk. While I have a personal relationship with God, and a cleric may, too, the cleric has a responsibility to guard and carry on the traditions of the Church. It doesn't matter what branch or belief it is, the cleric's responsibilities are to the Church. Lucas may have said something against the Church."

"Quite likely," Argolicus said, "considering how fervent he was about his new calling."

"Yes, but, murder as a response? Lucas was going away and from what we know he was not coming back. That's one reason his father was angry ..."

"It's all settled," Amalina said, coming into the peristylum with Maria by her side. Maria was smiling.

"What?" Argolicus asked, jarred out of his thinking.

"Maria will stay here until her wedding. We have plenty of room. It's not a problem. All we have to do ..."

"Mother, we can't. No. I promised Mattheus we'd stay out of their family affairs."

Maria's smile disappeared. Tears glistened at the corners of her eyes.

"No one should live in fear from their own family. You of all people should know injustice takes many forms."

Argolicus knew she was right. Maria needed protection. Why couldn't she find it somewhere else? He felt the box shrink around him. Now, his mother had given her word. For The People a word given was immutable, the basis of trust. Now he had given his word and so had his mother. They were at cross purposes.

"I gave my word." "And so did I," Amalina said. They stared at each other. Wiliarit and Nikolaos both scrutinized the painting. Maria's eyes began to well over above her trembling lip. The fountain burbled on in the sunlight until Amalina smiled.

"We can both keep our word. I will go with Maria to

gather some things and bring them back along with her maid. You will stay here, so you won't be involved."

"But, she will be here, in our house. I am the head of the household. Bartholomaeus will see me as interfering."

"Did you know Lucas was with Ebrimuth?" "No." "Then why would anyone need to know she is here?" Silence in the peristylum. "Good. That's settled then," Amalina said. She smiled and turned to Maria. "We'll have lunch and then go."

Maria smiled in relief and murmured, "Thank you." Amalina put her arm around Maria's shoulder and turned toward the kitchen.

"Mother," Argolicus said. "We will accompany you to the meadow and wait for you there to escort you back." Although he felt he was not keeping his word in a strict sense, he was relieved that they could keep Maria safe. Bartholomaeus was unpleasant and threatening.

"Lunch is an excellent idea," Wiliarit said. "What a beautiful day to eat here in the sunshine."

CHAPTER 8
AT BARTHOLOMAEUS' DOOR

The meadow was bright in the afternoon sun with more flowers than just a few days ago when they had found Lucas. Nikolaos brought the entire group through the woods where the trees had leafed out in a green canopy that thinned as they arrived in the meadow.

"I'll have to come back again when I am in search of flowers," Wiliarit said as he pushed wisps of forest undergrowth out of his way on the path. He held tight to the strap of his paint box. "This place is beautiful. Look how green the trees are. And this meadow. It's like the center of spring. I see how the ancient Romans loved their goddess Flora."

Maria said, "I love coming here. It's one place I will miss when I am married. This is where you found Lucas?" Her red cloak shone brilliant in the sun, matching the red meadow flowers.

"Yes," Argolicus, Nikolaos, and Wiliarit said in unison. Argolicus continued, "It was a gruesome sight. I wouldn't have recognized him except for the ring. You are better off missing that view of your brother."

"I saw him," Maria said. "I watched the slaves clean his body." She was silent for a moment. "But these flowers are like his spirit. That joy of life. That's what I miss. I was worried when he said he wanted to follow a monk, but now that I've spent time with Wiliarit I see that doesn't mean giving up a joy of life. I can understand him better now." She smiled at Wiliarit.

Wiliarit nodded. "I'll do more sketches while you are all at the villa." He opened his box and pulled out brushes.

"I've been thinking about that," Argolicus said. "Maria, I know you go for walks by yourself, but going to your father's house to retrieve your things... I think you may need protection. Wiliarit can stay here, but I will go up to the house. I won't go inside, but you'll know I am just outside the door."

Amalina said, "Thank you. Your kindness always comes through."

Argolicus never knew what to do when his mother complimented him. "All right, then. Let's head on. Wiliarit, we'll see you soon."

Wiliarit stooped over a tiny red flower. He stood up. "I'll be here." Then he crouched down to get a closer look.

The nearer they came to the villa, the more Argolicus' apprehension grew. Giving Maria safe harbor was right in one way. In another, he was in the midst of doing exactly what he said he would not do, meddle in the family affairs. But his mother had given her word. He refused to disappoint her and her right thinking.

In a few more minutes, they were outside the large villa. Among the busy servants and slaves bustling around the villa walls, a few servants and several elegantly equipped horses clustered toward the side of the imposing main door. The bishop, Argolicus thought. or some other wealthy noble.

Beyond the villa the fields bustled with slaves clearing for spring planting. He realized why Nikolaos had been busy in his personal herb garden setting out new plants. Herbs for curing. Herbs for healing.

They gathered at the edge of the woods. All of them looking at the villa walls.

Amalina wrapped her large *pala* around her shoulders, took Maria's hand and led her to the side work entrance where they disappeared. Argolicus and Nikolaos found a large tree and waited in the shade by the trunk. Nikolaos pulled out a small book. Argolicus groaned inside. Quiet time was always a time for instruction or practice even in times as tense as this. Argolicus hoped his mother would successfully get Maria out without being spotted. He thought of her as a matron, but realized she was brave in her own way, ready to stand up for her beliefs.

Argolicus was about to share his thoughts with Nikolaos to interrupt any intentions of practicing Greek. But, the eldest brother Mattheus suddenly stood in the main doorway, his face grim above his silks.

"Inside," Mattheus called, waving his arm toward the door. No coming to meet them or polite greeting. "Come inside now. This is the end of your meddling."

Nikolaos put away the book and followed Argolicus into the atrium of the big villa.

Inside the room with its brightly painted walls and colorful mosaic floor, Amalina looked on stoically as Bartholomaeus gripped Maria's arm. Maria was not in tears even though her cheek had a big red patch. She looked at Argolicus with quiet desperation.

Seeing the red patch on the girl's cheek was all it took for Argolicus to side with his mother. Bartholomaeus was like many men, rough with his family. Maria was in danger from her own father. He'd seen it before, the hitting always got worse, never lessened. He wanted her to stay safe and felt powerless to do anything. He looked at his mother who wore her outrage face, lips pressed tight, eyes flashing.

Matheus said to his father, "Here he is. I knew he was behind all this." He went to stand behind his father alongside Marcus. Both brothers scowled. "You gave me your word. Some noble you are. Your word is worth nothing. How you managed in Rome is beyond me. We're not happy you are back. Your family is trouble."

Bartholomaeus glanced at Matheus, released Maria's arm, roughly thrusting it away.

Down the passageway to the peristylum Argolicus saw Bishop Braga surrounded by several deacons. He paced in his stiff-gaited way up and down trailed by his retinue along the marble pathway next to spring flowers in the garden. The fracas with Maria had interrupted whatever the argument was he'd had with Bartholomaeus.

Before Bartholomaeus could respond, Amalina spoke, her eyes flashing blue ice but her voice calm. "No, he was against this. It was my idea. My idea to keep a woman from being traumatized, threatened, and hit. You may think of us as barbarians and heretics, but women have an equal place with men." She stood tall, her clear words without rancor.

There was silence. Argolicus marveled at his mother's aplomb, startled and grateful for her intervention. In the far room, he saw Bishop Braga stop his pacing to listen as his deacons stopped speaking, ears turned toward the atrium.

Then Bartholomaeus answered. "Whatever you are, whatever your beliefs, you cannot meddle in our family affairs." He turned to Argolicus. "You go away to Rome and think you can come back and fix everything by trying to control other people's lives. I am pater familias here. What I do in my family is my prerogative. I am a true believer following the traditions of the true church. Women have their place and men lead. I lead. Maria is marrying into a good family. She is blessed. A spinster like her needs to marry..."

Argolicus had heard enough. He held out his hand. "Mother, come. We can do nothing here."

Amalina crossed to Argolicus and took his hand. He could feel her trembling with anger. He gripped her hand to reassure her and felt the anger throbbing in her palm. But, before he left he had more to say.

"Maria, I will keep my word." He hoped she understood that he meant to continue looking for Lucas' murderer. She looked at him as she rubbed her arm. He thought he saw a slight nod. He turned to Bartholomaeus. "I will keep my word. I will not meddle in your family affairs."

Bartholomaeus stood as still as a statue. Beyond him in the peristylum Braga and the deacons had stopped any pretense of not listening, their eyes glued on Argolicus.

Holding his mother's hand and followed by Nikolaos, Argolicus strode toward the door.

Outside, they headed back toward the meadow. Amalina trembled in rage.

"What a disgusting man," she said. "He hit Maria. I saw him." She shook her head. "Your father was a Roman. He was nothing like that." She wrapped her *pala* around her shoulders. The blue shawl matched the color of her eyes, but not the icy glare.

"I've seen truly evil men in Rome. Yes, Father was exceptional and we are fortunate. But, Bartholomaeus is full of himself and misguided. Unpleasant but not evil."

"He feels evil to me. What happened to that *civitas* Romans are so proud of? That's an older tradition than the church. It feels like Bartholomaeus picks the traditions that serve his sense of himself. Proud and rigid without courtesy." She was far from calming down. "And what about our own king's *civilitas* where we all are to live in harmony? What about that?"

"Mother, we are far from Ravenna. You see in everyday life here that what the king says has little sway on common occurrences. We were fortunate. I was fortunate to have you and Father. Your were fortunate to marry a man who believed in those values. Bartholomaeus isn't like Father. Most men are not like Father was.

"That man is a brute," Amalina said, rubbing her arm as if to rid herself of the man. Her *pala* slipped, and she pulled it around her again.

"People's beliefs lead them down strange paths of righteousness. Self-righteousness. That's Bartholomaeus. Evil people believe in their twisted thinking that they are doing the right thing. But he isn't evil. He's misguided in his thinking. I've met evil people. They care for no one. Bartholomaeus cares for his family, just in his way. Now where is that path to the meadow?"

"Over there," Nikolaos said, pointing to the thick greenery of the woods. He led them into the shadowy woods where twigs crackled under their feet as they walked.

CHAPTER 9
MEADOW CROSSING

❦❧

In the darkening woods, Argolicus, Amalina, and Nikolaos trod in defeat toward the meadow and Wiliarit.

"Was it bad judgment?" Amalina asked. "I was trying to protect her. I think all I did was make it worse."

Argolicus sighed. "No, Mother. A caring heart is not bad judgment. But interfering in family matters doesn't work. I supported you knowing full well that intervention is intrusion. Our families are not destined to be on friendly terms."

"If anything, we've widened the gap," Amalina sad. "Harboring Maria was a noble intent but a bad idea."

"We've spent years without contact. Now we can go back to not interacting with the family. I have one last task and then..."

"What do you mean one last task? Didn't you just agree that we'll keep our families separate?"

"I gave my word to Maria. I must find who killed Lucas."

Nikolaos kept silent leading the way through the thick underbrush. The shadows grew deeper as the afternoon headed toward dusk. They walked on until they could see the sunlight on the flower-filled meadow.

Wiliarit sat cross legged on the ground, intent on the same star-shaped tiny red flower. Nikolaos cried a greeting. Wiliarit began putting his brushes and paints back in his box.

"I wondered when you'd..." He looked behind Argolicus and Amalina. "Where's Maria?"

"It's a long story. Remember how at the beginning you

warned me not to get involved?" Argolicus said. "You were right. I'll tell you as we walk."

He heard a twig break and turned around. Three hooded ruffians broke out of the woods just as Nikolaos cried, "Hup!"

Argolicus centered his weight on flexed knees as he felt energy surge through his body. It was as if all his senses were on alert. Without thinking his fingers tingled. He heard each of the hooligans' quiet footsteps. His heart beat in strong, intense rhythm.

Wiliarit put down his paint box and reached into his robe. He looked at Argolicus with dilated eyes and nodded.

Nikolaos moved first, hurtling through the air toward the first thug. He clung to the huge man. The tutor's feet waved in the air as he sent blows up to the thug's face.

Argolicus rushed toward the second hooded figure shaking a club in threatening gestures, his arms up in a defense and ready to send out the first punch. Argolicus stopped, stepped forward to put his weight behind his punch to the man's abdomen. The man doubled up with an "oof" of surprise. Jolted by the blow he dropped the wooden club and leaned in to punch back. His arm didn't reach Argolicus who danced back preparing his next strike. The thug moved closer. Argolicus was ready with his defenses. He ducked below the blow, then warded off the next blow with his left arm while landing another punch to the man's jaw with his right fist.

Nikolaos leaped off the big man. Dashed behind and leaped on again throwing his arm around the big man's neck in a stranglehold. With his other arm he punched the man repeatedly in the ear and side of his head. The thug leaned over in pain. He tried to shake off the slave. Nikolaos held on and continued his relentless blows to the head.

Wiliarit pulled out a leather wrapped sap that swung from a leather strap and headed toward the third thug who brandished a club above his head. The thug was unprepared for the reach and swing of the metal-filled leather weapon in the large monk's hand. Wiliarit struck the man's arm held high with the club. A crack resounded through the meadow as the leather sap hit.

Somehow the thug hit Argolicus on his left side. A sear of pain shot through his ribs. He punched back blindly.

Unphased, the thug, tried a second blow to his side.

This time Argolicus had his arm ready to block the blow. And he gained control of his senseless punching to land a blow squarely on the man's jaw. The thug stepped back, shook his head, and fell to the ground.

Amalina was by his side. "Enough of this man. I'll help Wiliarit. You go to Nikolaos." She pulled a long dagger from her belt as she rushed to Wiliarit.

Wiliarit and the thug were grappling in a wrestle on the ground. Each man trying to strangle the other.

Argolicus charged toward the large thug with Nikolaos on his back. The thug tried to punch Nikolaos, but the small slave clung behind his head where the man couldn't reach.

Argolicus hit him first with his right fist. He followed with a jab from his left to the man's jaw. Stunned, the thug staggered back.

Before Argolicus could think, Nikolaos let go. He rushed to the man's front and delivered a blow to the middle of the man's chest. The air rushed out as the man fell to the ground stunned. He looked up in amazement at the tiny slave in front of him as he gasped for breath.

Amalina tossed the dagger to her left hand. She picked up the leather sap lying beside the two wrestling men. She swung the sap in the air from the leather strap. She stood over the writhing figures and waited for the thug to move within reach. Then she swung the weighted sap on the man's head. He collapsed under Wiliarit.

Amalina ran toward her *pala* piled in a heap on the meadow grass. She ripped long strips from the shawl.

Argolicus realized what she was doing. He took a strip and tied the hands of the thug who had fought Wiliarit. When he was finished, he bound the big thug who could not shake off Nikolaos. Amalina ripped more strips. Finally Argolicus bound the hands of the thug who had passed out from the blow to the jaw.

"Now," said Argolicus, standing over the three men. "Who sent you?"

The two who were conscious spoke together. "It was a man..." "He didn't give us his name..."

"One at a time," Argolicus said.

Wiliarit was up from the ground. Amalina handed him the sap. "Useful tool, brother." Wiliarit smiled.

Argolicus waited. None of the three men spoke. Argolicus pointed at the largest thug. "Tell me."

"He was...he didn't say his name. He...he had money."

"He gave you money to find us?"

"Yes, he said you would come toward the meadow."

The third thug woke up, sat up, shook his head, and stared at his bound hands.

"And, what did he want you to do?"

"You. He described you. Noble with a monk and a woman from The People."

"And?"

"You. He told us to get rid of you. He promised more money when we returned."

Wiliarit put his arm around Amalina. She leaned onto his shoulder.

"Describe this man."

"He was a slave, like that little devil there." He pointed to Nikolaos. "Well dressed. A clean tunic. Medium tall. Brown hair. Ordinary house slave."

"Who sent him?"

"He...he didn't say."

"And, where were you? How did he know how to find you?"

"We're always outside the bishop's palace. You know how it is. No steady work. But sometimes we get jobs."

"Like this one?"

"Well, not exactly like this one. Usually, it's, you know, someone who owes the bishop. We go to collect." He nodded toward the other two thugs.

"Have you ever done something like this, before?"

The thug looked down, then glanced at the other two. "Well...not all three of us."

"What do you mean not all three? Just you?"

"I'm the biggest. I..."

"I see." Argolicus felt he was close to a revelation. "Recently? Recently anything like this?"

The thug looked out at the forest trees, over at Wiliarit's paint box, down at his feet. He mumbled, "Just one."

"Here, in this meadow?"

"How did you...? You couldn't..."

"Here. In this meadow?"

"Y,.. Y,.. Yes. Just one man. A poor one. I did what I was asked."

"Which was?"

"Bring back his bag. Hurt him." The big thug shifted on the ground.

"And you did? You hurt him and took back the bag."

The thug shifted his eyes and said, "Yes. Hurt him. Then grabbed the bag and ran."

"You did more than hurt him." The thug nodded his head and looked away at the trees again. "I heard. I didn't mean... It just happened."

"I want to understand," Argolicus said. "You were not told to kill him?"

"He didn't use the word. No. But, he..." The thug searched for a word.

"He implied. He meant that hurting could be killing."

"Yes, yes. You understand. I mean I hardly ever get instructions to kill. But people, some people, know I can rough people up. And, what was that word?"

"Imply."

"Yes, sometimes the instructions imply."

A breeze rustled in the trees. The grass and flowers nodded in the meadow. Everyone was silent waiting for Argolicus to decide. Argolicus felt like hitting the man. But he checked himself because the man was just a thug. and not a smart one. He needed to know who had hired the thug.

"This man, the man who gave you the instructions. Tell me more about him. Anything you remember. Anything at all."

The man shook his head. "He was just a slave. I told you."

"He had good shoes," the thug in front of Amalina said, eyeing her dagger.

"Good shoes? What do you mean?" Argolicus asked, turning toward the man. He didn't know what this meant but maybe it was something.

"They weren't fancy, no embroidery, but they were good shoes. New leather. Supple. No blisters for that man." The thug looked at his feet out in front of him. "See these? Stiff. Even though they're worn, they are stiff. But that slave is taken care of, I can tell you that. I used to work leather before these hard times. Those shoes were good shoes."

"Anything else?"

The three men looked at each other.

The big thug shrugged his shoulders. "He was from here. I guess that just adds to his being ordinary. You know how slaves come from all over the world? Well, this one had no accent. He looked like us...well, except for being better dressed. I mean he was just an ordinary man, but from Bruttia. He was easy to understand."

Argolicus was getting bits and pieces but nothing that distinguished the man who had paid the thugs. "Alright, let's get you to the promagistrate. Nikolaos, lead the way."

Amalina loosened the ties around the thugs' feet to hobble them. Wiliarit got the men to stand up one by one. Argolicus gathered the thugs' clubs and wrapped them in what was left of Amalina's shawl so it served as a large bag. Then they all headed through the woods toward home. The sun was getting low in the sky. The trees cast dark shadows and Argolicus was glad Nikolaos knew the way.

❧

At the villa, they gathered the men in the courtyard until the promagistrate arrived. A kitchen slave came out with soup for everyone. Another slave set up torch lights around the courtyard against the gathering evening. They waited in silence.

As the shock of the attack wore off, and they were all safe at home with the thugs apprehended, Argolicus felt the pains of the attack and muscle soreness from fighting. The knuckles on both hands ached. A dull pain burned his left shoulder. But, what bothered him was his frustration at finding the person who had instigated the attack and, now that he knew, Lucas' murder. They had apprehended the thugs, but he didn't know the person with the intent. The men in front of him were merely living instruments, like the clubs they had wielded.

He glanced at Wiliarit who had a red welt on his cheek. Amalina's pale cheeks seemed to highlight the wrinkles around her mouth and eyes. Nikolaos, standing by the practice swords they'd used this morning, was rubbing his arm. The practice swords. Without that constant practice, Argolicus would have been unprepared for the attack. The king's law forbade Romans from carrying arms. Only The People could carry arms. He'd been fortunate to have his mother and Wiliarit with him...and prepared. More than fortunate that Nikolaos made him practice. Suddenly, he had a sense of how they could have ended up left in the meadow like Lucas.

He heard horses approaching and men's voices. The promagistrate and his deputies appeared in the courtyard. They rounded up the three thugs. As they led them away, the big thug turned around. "He had a missing tooth...on the bottom."

CHAPTER 10
PAINTING A NEW PICTURE

The figures on the frescos seemed to move in the flickering lamplight in the triclinium. Reclining on the dining bench relaxed Argolicus' sore muscles, and the food on the table smelled delicious.

"I was ravenous," Wiliarit said, dipping a spoon into the herbed lentil soup. They spoke in Their Language since it was only the three of them. "It's been a long time since I've been in a fight." He rubbed at a cut over his eye.

Argolicus laughed. "I haven't had a real fight since boyhood. This was different. They planned to harm us. I don't think killing was out of the question. As the man said, it was implied." His raw knuckles stretched in pain as he lifted his spoon.

"But why?" Amalina asked, signalling for the next dish. "Was helping Maria worth killing? That family. Bartholomaeus is not a nice man. Killing us wouldn't accomplish anything. He has his daughter back."

Argolicus looked at the rough patch on her cheek that would soon be a large scab. The wrinkles that radiated from the corners of her eyes, always associated with smiles, indicated that age was not a barrier to courage.

"I don't know," Argolicus said. "I've sent a message to him that Lucas' killer is apprehended and with the promagistrate in town. He will have to resolve it in his own way. But for us, it doesn't solve the problem. If someone wants us out of the way, they can hire different thugs. We haven't found the real murderer. The one who had Lucas killed. The one who sent thugs after us." He tried shifting away from the aches again without success.

"Ah, tuna," Wiliarit said, as the fish in lovage and mint sauce arrived on the table. He put down his spoon and waited as the kitchen slave put a steaming piece of fish on a plate. "Do you think it's personal, against us, or some provincial rebellion against The People?" He tucked into the tuna with vigorous bites.

"In some ways it doesn't matter," Argolicus said. "A threat is a threat. And Mother is right. Why? I suspect it has something to do with Lucas. But what? What we do know is that Lucas is dead, the icon is missing, and we were attacked." He shifted on the couch trying to get comfortable, but the aches just shifted with his movement.

"That poor girl," Amalina said, taking a larger than usual portion of fish. "When is her wedding? She can't get away from all that fast enough."

"You were the one that talked to her. I thought you knew. Isn't it in a few weeks?" Argolicus felt his obligation pressing in. He might never keep his promise to Maria.

Amalina nodded her head. "It can't be soon enough."

"We will stay away from that family," Argolicus said. "I'll keep looking for who wanted Lucas dead because they threatened us, too. But, unless we determine that a family member hired those thugs, we stay away." A bitterness rose in his throat. How old allegiances had come back to strike him and his family.

Amalina and Wiliarit nodded.

"Where is Nikolaos?"

"Now that dinner has been prepared, he's busy in the kitchen, cooking up remedies for us," Amalina replied, her cheek stretching with the stiff red patch.

"Ugh," Wiliarit said. "I hope we don't have to drink some vile concoction from his herb garden."

"Those vile concoctions work," Argolicus said in defense of his tutor. "He knows plants. Isn't that why you are here?"

"Yes, yes." Wiliarit conceded. "But still..."

"Do you want to wait to have the fruit?" Amalina asked with complete deadpan, summoning years of sibling communication.

"No, no. Fruit next," Wiliarit said. "We can drink honeyed wine after any of Nikolaos' potions."

After dinner, Nikolaos gathered them all on the benches in the peristylum. The night was warm for late March. Slaves lit up the area with torches.

Nikolaos had prepared poultices for wounds and, yes, a tangy, but not bitter, herbal tisane for them all.

In the quiet moments while his patients were under his care, he pulled out a book and began reading. "Nature is pliable, obedient. And the logos that governs it has no reason to do evil. It knows no evil, does none, and causes harm to nothing. It dictates al beginnings and al endings." He paused, glanced at all the visible wounds, and continued. "Just that you do the right thing. The rest doesn't matter."

"I could do the right thing now, rest," Wiliarit said, interrupting the reading and speaking in Latin for the benefit of Nikolaos. "But what burns my mind is who hired those thugs." He touched the poultice over his wound. "They did this, but their intent was worse."

Argolicus nodded raising his soaking knuckles with the cup to sip the tisane. Not as vile as expected.

"Think of them all," Argolicus said. "Bartholomaeus, Braga, Mattheus, Marcus, why would they really care about the icon? What upset them all was his new belief. The way he countered the traditions and hierarchies of the Church by supporting a belief system that had to do with personal decisions. Lucas was a defiant departure from tradition." Somehow, sitting on the bench made his aches feel better. The dining couch. He wondered about sleep in bed. Would it be as uncomfortable as reclining to eat?

"I agree," Amalina said, taking a sip of tisane and making a face. "Nikolaos, what is this?"

"Surely, it's time for some honeyed wine," Wiliarit said, taking a gulp of tisane to make it disappear.

"Have you finished your drink?" Nikolaos asked, looking up from the book. His instruction from Marcus Aurelius was not keeping anyone's attention. He closed the book.

Everyone nodded yes. Wiliarit tipped up his cup for one last sip. Then he set the cup down. "It wasn't as awful as I'd expected."

Nikolaos ignored him and continued, "Each of them has enough money to hire a thug, even a band of thugs, to do their dirty work. Since we know the same thugs were used against Lucas and against us, we only need to find the one person behind them."

"Well, that goes without saying," Argolicus replied, feeling irritable with his aching body and scored knuckles. "But, I will not give up."

Wiliarit said, "I think I know. Well, I have a strong suspicion."

They all looked at him expectantly. A servant brought out a tray with cups and a pitcher of honeyed wine.

"Ah, inspiration," Wiliarit said, reaching for a cup.

"Don't make us wait, Uncle. Tell us your idea."

"It's like the sketches I've been doing. You have a subject, in this case, all the people who might have wished Lucas harm, but when you start the next sketch, you see a detail that had escaped your notice before..."

"Stop," Amalina said in her older sister voice. "Skip the theoretical analogy and get to your idea."

"Let me put it less artistically," Wiliarit continued without missing a beat. "Solving a puzzle, like who killed Lucas, isn't so much about finding tidbits of clues that can point in any direction, it's about knowing what to look for. And, you may scoff," he looked at Amalina, "but it's like painting a new picture of the same subject."

Argolicus, determined to quell a decades-old sibling squabble, said, "Paint the picture."

"We've been focused on Church traditions and how Lucas antagonized everyone with his newfound faith. But we've overlooked something equally strong, the hierarchy inside the Church. Instead of looking at which Church or Church leader holds the correct belief, we can look at the structure inside the Church. I work with this structure when I make books for prelates."

"I don't understand," Nikolaos said as he peeked under Amalina's poultice to check her wound.

"We've been basing our thoughts on the outside traditions, but we need to look at the inside traditions. You can't imagine how complicated it is in Constantinople. Rome is nothing. And, here, for Squillace, the structure is the same."

Argolicus could see his mother was about to reprimand Wiliarit again. He spoke before she could. "Explain. I'm not sure I understand either."

"Unlike a priest, loyal to the Church, the deacon's obligation is to the bishop. If the bishop orders something, the deacon performs. Braga could express a wish or even mumble a discontent and a zealous deacon eager for advancement who heard him could carry out an act unknown to the bishop. Braga need not be involved personally. The deacon might mention later an act he had done in order to curry favor and gain personal prestige with the bishop. This is the picture. While priests are bound to the Church, deacons are bound by oath to serve the bishop. Theoretically, they carry out the benevolence of the bishop through daily actions. They perform administrative duties, like a merchant's clerks. And if the bishop expresses a desire, they make it happen in the everyday world."

"So, the man with the missing tooth came from a deacon, not the bishop?" Amalina asked, sipping at her cup of wine.

"The bishop, but through a deacon. The man with the missing tooth never spoke to the bishop. He received an order and carried it out. All this could happen without the bishop's knowledge. Of course, this is a speculative thought."

Nikolaos approached Wiliarit to check his wound, but the monk waved him away. The monk took a long sip of wine.

"That's an interesting theory, but why couldn't he come from someone in Bartholomaeus' family? I don't see how we've narrowed it down to the bishop or a deacon," Amalina said, determine to poke a hole in her brother's elaborate analogy.

Nikolaos fussed with Argolicus knuckles, patting the poultice around the edges. Argolicus winced. They still went in circles around Lucas' murder.

"So, let's start with the Bishop. We can't go to Bartholomaeus house. Truthfully, I don't want to see him again. Uncle, can you make one last visit before you leave for Constantinople?"

Wiliarit nodded, then took a gulp of honeyed wine.

Wiliarit took time out from sketching plants to paint a representation of Ignatius of Antioch sailing on a boat to Rome writing letters to his flock.

"Usually he's represented with the lions grinding his bones, but Braga doesn't seem like a man who wants to think about martyrdom."

"It's ready?" Argolicus asked. "And you have an appointment?"

"Yes, this afternoon."

"Thank you for doing this, Uncle. We have no idea if this will reveal anything at all."

"You gave your word to Maria. Plus, I know you. You don't give up." He put his large arm around Argolicus' shoulder.

This time there was no visit to the treasures. Braga met them in the sparse *salutorium*. Seated on his bishop's chair, he listened to Wiliarit as he displayed his painting of Ignatius.

Wiliarit handed the vellum sheet with the painting to the bishop.

"So, the book would have the letters of Ignatius written in a fine script with illustrations, much like this one. You can control the price in accordance with how many illustrations you want added to the letters."

Braga squinted at the sheet, his stubby ringed fingers

handling the sheet with care. With his other hand he motioned to several deacons standing at the side of the big empty room. "You have read this Ignatius?"

The answers came back in mumbles. "No." "I don't read, Father." "No, but it would be a worthy addition."

A young deacon came into the room, brown robes hanging over a thin frame. "Your visitor." He announced.

Braga frowned, his snub nose wrinkling. "He is early. But bring him in."

The deacon returned followed by Bartholomaeus. He swept in with his silks flowing. Frowned at Argolicus and Wiliarit, went to the bishop, fell on his knee, and kissed the bishop's ring snuggled among the jewelled fingers.

The bishop said, "Let me finish here. I'm considering adding a book to the collection." He held out the vellum sheet to Bartholomaeus.

"For your library?" Bartholomaeus asked. "What will it be? Who is this?" He pointed to the figure on the boat.

While the bishop told Bartholomaeus about the early Church fathers and Ignatius in particular, Argolicus looked at the deacons arranged around the room. Was Wiliarit right, could the murderous plotter be one of them? They all looked just as committed as Wiliarit did in his monk's robes. If it was one of the deacons, how would he discover which one? Had he set himself up for a fool's errand? And, now, Bartholomaeus was here. There was bound to be trouble.

The entry door opened again. This time a servant entered, not a deacon. With soft steps not to disturb the bishop, he sidled around the edges of the room until he stood by a deacon. Argolicus recognized the deacon as the one who had taken them on the tour of the treasures. What was his name? Mico. Yes. And now he was in a whispered conversation with a servant, a servant with very nice shoes, Argolicus noticed. The whispered conversation continued. Braga looked at them briefly, scowled, and then continued on with his explanation. The servant smiled, exposing his teeth, and turned to leave.

"Your Grace," Argolicus interrupted. "With your permission, could I have a word?"

Braga stopped. Argolicus saw his face pass from annoyance to curiosity back to annoyance. A strand of his oiled hair had escaped over his forehead as he bent over the sketch. He pushed it back.

"Yes," Braga said. "Is it about the book? I think I have made my decision."

"No," Argolicus answered as he walked toward the deacon Mico. "I have a question for your deacon."

Mico squirmed in his plain robe, glanced at the servant, and left his spot by the wall. "Yes?"

But Braga cut them short. "What is it? I was just getting ready to give the talented monk his answer."

Argolicus with no explanation turned to the deacon. "This is your servant?"

The servant tried to keep his composure but sent a worried glance at Mico who answered, "He belongs to the palace...all of us."

Argolicus turned to the servant. "This man," he pointed to the deacon, "gave you money to hire men outside the palace?"

The servant glanced down, up at the deacon Mico, and down again. "Many times."

"And the last two times?"

Bartholomaeus spoke up. "What's this about? You seem to meddle wherever you go."

Argolicus pointed to the servant who seemed to want to disappear. "This, as you say, this man and this deacon," he turned to Mico, "are about the death of your son."

Braga dropped the sketch. "What is he saying, Mico?"

"Is this true? How?" Bartholomaeus asked.

"Your Grace," Mico said, casting his eyes down. "I heard you. I heard you say what a pestilence that man was, how you wanted him to disappear."

"What are you saying?" Braga stood, his face flushed red. "You hired men, in my name to kill that young man?"

"Not in your name," Mico answered, his voice rising. "I hoped to make your desire a fact. I wanted to please you. I thought you would..."

Bartholomaeus strode across the empty *salutorium*. He hit the deacon and then the servant. Then he pummeled the deacon. "You! My son! My boy. You. You. You." With each word he struck Mico who fell to the floor. Bartholomaeus lifted his leg to kick.

"Enough," Braga said, his voice filling the big room.

Bartholomaeus stood back his face filled with fury.

"Mico, you have dishonored your calling, my name, and the Church. You are no longer bound to the duties and obligations you incurred upon ordination. Go, take off your robes and wait in the entry room for the promagistrate. And, you," he turned to the servant whose mouth, open in stunned surprise, showed his missing tooth, "you will go with this man and wait with him for the promagistrate."

The two men slunk from the room. The bishop returned to his ornate chair. The other deacons stood silently their faces filled with mixtures of surprise, condemnation, and shame.

Bartholomaeus stood with a similar combination of surprise and shame. "Your Grace, I must put off our business for today."

Braga nodded. "There is no rush. We have time and faith to begin our project. May your soul be at peace with this new knowledge."

Wiliarit stooped to pick up the vellum sheet. He handed it back to the bishop.

Bartholomaeus turned to Argolicus. "You accomplished something I prayed for every day, the discovery of who killed Lucas. Our faiths will always separate us, but I will always be in your debt."

"Tell Maria I kept my word."

❧

Days later the carter loaded boxes onto a cart as Amalina and Wiliarit hugged their goodbyes. Wiliarit let go of his sister.

"Nikolaos, forays with you helped me complete all my sketches. Your knowledge," he shook his head. "I would have been lost without it. And, you," he said turning to Argolicus. "Our peaceful discussions turned into something quite lively. City life will seem calm after this." He held his arms wide open and then embraced Argolicus. He pushed back and said to the carter, "Ready."

As he settled into the seat beside the carter, he said to Argolicus, "I left something for you on your desk" The carter called to the horses, and they were off down the hill.

In his study, Argolicus found a sheet of vellum with an inscription surrounded by small, red, yellow, and blue meadow flowers. *Do the right thing. The rest does not matter.*

"Mother," he called. "Your brother is astounding."

Amalina appeared at the door. "He is. But now it's time to talk about what you will do with the rest of your life."

Argolicus sighed.

GLOSSARY

Glossary

Acacian division - The prelate of Constantinople, Acacius.
advised the Byzantine emperor Zeno to issue the Henotikon
edict in 482 C.E., in which Nestorius and Eutyches were
condemned, the twelve chapters of Cyril of Alexandria
accepted, and the Chalcedon Definition ignored. This effort
to shelve the dispute over the Orthodoxy of the Council of
Chalcedon eventually came to nothing but was not ended
until 319 C.E.

Atrium - The formal reception room at the front of a
Roman home. Members of the family received guests here.
The roof had an opening in the middle so the room was
exposed to weather. Most atriums also had a pool of water in
the middle which captured rain.

Civilitas - A concept of civility and fairness proclaimed by
King Theodoric, to bear on all relations between and among
people under his rule.

Civitas - The Roman law that bound citizens together in a
common agreement binding all Roman citizens.

Garum - A sauce made by fermenting salted fish offal for

months in the open air. Considered a delicacy and common on all tables.

Pala - A large shawl (approximately 12 feet by 5 feet) originally worn by men and women. At the time of the story, a garment worn by women.

Peristylum - A large room at the back of a Roman home. The opening in the roof was larger than that of the atrium. The area was decorated with plants and flowers, often a fountain, and was a family gathering place.

Salutorium - The official reception room for a bishop. Furnishings were sparse except for the bishop's chair. Visitors stood while the bishop sat.

Triclinium - The dining room. Furnished with tables set in the shape of a U. Diners reclined on benches, often padded, to eat. A diner would lean on an elbow to reach food with the opposite hand.

AFTERWORD

The Dioscorides was translated into Latin with the title De Materia Medica. The book in the story is the oldest extant copy and was presented the Emperor Anicius Olybrius' daughter, Juliana Anica, around 512 C.E. The book is currently housed in the Austrian National Library in Vienna. The book includes hundreds of illustrations some of which occupy Wiliarit in the story.

Although Wiliarit is credited with the creation of The Gothic Bible (Codex Argenteus at Uppsala University) and other books of the time, he is not directly connected with the Dioscorides. I imagined him creating the book and needing Nikolaos' help.

According to Patrick Amory's *People and identity in Ostrogothic Italy 480-554*, Wiliarit was probably a monk as well as a book maker. I reduced the probability to a certainty and created his familial relationship with Argolicus.

At the time of the story, monks both Arian and Trinitarian either lived alone or in loose communities based on the tradition of the Desert Fathers like Anthony. At this time, Benedict lived alone in a cave following that tradition. He had yet to form his monastery or create his Rules. His connection with Lucas comes from my imagination.

Modern readers should understand that religion and politics were intertwined. Feelings ran strong about the nature of Christ and colored daily activities and interactions in a way it's difficult to comprehend today.

The Henotikon was a document issued by the Emperor Zeno in 491 C.E. in an attempt to unify the various sects (heresies) of the Christian Church. It caused a schism between East and West and was not settled until 519 C.E. seven years after the time of this story. Bartholomaeus may seem extreme, but he was current. His iron fist over his family was within his rights as pater familias.

Amalina's feelings about women come from her Ostrogoth heritage where women had equal rights with men, within tribal law.

According to James J. O'Donnell in, the most upwardly mobil The Ruin of the Roman Empiree sector at this time were members of the Church. Braga is a man of his times.

I am grateful to James J. O'Donnell for his personal encouragement when I first began my journey with Argolicus and the reign of Theodoric.

Historical fiction is built on a combination of history and the author's imagination. All historical errors are mine and mine alone.

Zara Altair

ENJOY THIS BOOK? YOU CAN MAKE A BIG DIFFERENCE.

Thank you for reading *The Vellum Scribe.*

You wouldn't be here if you didn't like a good mystery and diving into another time.

Building a relationship with my readers is the very best thing about writing.

Reviews are the most powerful tools in my arsenal when it comes to getting attention to my books. Much as I'd like to, I don't have the financial muscle of a big New York publisher. I can't take out full-page ads or put posters on subways.

(Not yet, anyway.) But I have something more powerful and effective than that, and those publishers would kill to get their hands on.

A committed and loyal bunch of readers. Honest reviews of my books help bring them to the attention of other readers.

If you have enjoyed any one of the Argolicus Mysteries I would be very grateful if you could spend just five minutes leaving a review on the book's review page. It can be as short as you like.

Thank you very much!

Want to learn more about Argolicus? Join the Fans of Argolicus. http://bit.ly/ArgolicusReader. You'll receive a free copy of the Argolicus mystery *The Peach Widow* where Argolicus sets his legal knowledge against avaricious brothers. Plus, you'll receive personal updates on new Argolicus stories and what's happening in my writer world.

ABOUT THE AUTHOR

Zara Altair combines mystery with a bit of adventure in the Argolicus mysteries. *The Vellum Scribe* is another story in the series of mysteries based in southern Italy at the time of the Ostrogoth rule of Italy under Theodoric the Great. Italians (Romans) and Goths live under one king while the Roman Empire is ruled from Constantinople. At times the cultures clash, but Argolicus uses his wit, sometimes with help from his tutor Nikolaos, to provide justice in a province far from the King's court.

Zara Altair lives in Beaverton, Oregon. Her approach to writing is to present the puzzle and let Argolicus and Nikolaos find the solution encountering a bit of adventure and some humor in their search. Her stories are rich in historical detail based on years of research.

Stay in Touch
www.zaraaltair.com
zara@zaraaltair.com

The Peach Widow

Look for The Grain Merchant coming next.